A
TASTE
OF
SOMETHING
ELSE

A TASTE OF SOMETHING ELSE

A NOVEL BY
BLACK PATRICK

BLACK PATRICK
PUBLISHING
LOS ANGELES

This is a work of fiction. Any similarities to people sharing the same name as you appear within these pages because the author has a sick sense of humor. Be grateful you may or may not be somewhat interesting to someone somewhere. Don't freak out, it's all going to be okay.

blackpatrick.com

ISBN 979-8-8692-4524-3

1 3 5 7 9 10 8 6 4 2

Printed in the United States of America. Motherfucker.

Published 2024
First edition published 2024.

BLACK PATRICK
PUBLISHING
LOS ANGELES

Somebody put something in my drink.
—Joey Ramone

Ivy & Black Patrick. On acid.
Shibuya, Tokyo, Japan.

CONTENTS

BLACK PATRICK

"I did what I knew best. I worked hard. If somebody'd told me how to give up I think I probably would've. But I didn't know, so I kept going."
—Black Patrick

PART 1
DIG IT

ONE

GUITAR MEETS TURKEY

MOUNT WASHINGTON

"DO YOU THINK TENNIS WILL SOLVE THAT?"
As the sun set on our little version of human civilization, Felix and his wife, Irma, maintained a spirited yet unhappy marriage. A small seed fertilized by wave after wave of misery germinated in the dark and musty place known as Irma's brain then sprouted to produce a crop of primo problem-solving tennis-related information on the day we all gathered to celebrate genocide.

I snuck past the domestic dispute in the courtyard, through the front door, and down the stairs into the safe zone. Wilson rarely left the man cave under his house. Who could blame him? Stripper pole, Les Paul, Marshall stack, kegerator…

Wilson closed one eye, squinted, and said, "Patrick! Happy Thanksgiving!" when he realized I was the one pouring shots at his bar.

"That's what they all say. I sold my Hendrix Strat yesterday."

"Why?"

"I needed drugs."

"That's what they all say. Who'd you sell it to?"

"Some loser from Studio City. Craigslist. He just sent me a text asking for a $75 refund. Check this out:"

Hi Patrick, went through the hendrix strat, plays great but you mentioned that you bought this new from Sweetwater but there are some parts that aren't original to this guitar. Tremolo arm is a David gilmour style arm, not a big issue but it doesn't seat properly in the bridge, so basically unusable
Back trem plate is not original, I actually don't use these covers so it doesn't matter to me
The major issue is that pickups are not the 65 American vintage that come with this guitar from the
factory. Attached are pics of the pickups in the vs what they should be. The pickups in the guitar are "246" couldn't figure what those came from but the 65 pups that should be in there should have grey back plates, etc.

Wondering if you can either send me a partial refund, or I can return the guitar for a full refund.
If partial refund, I can give you the trem arm, non original pickups, and back for resale. Those parts all total up to about $180 but I'd be happy with a $100 refund and you get the parts or $75 refund and I'll sell the parts off, either way, please let me know. Thanks

Wilson knew the answer, but he asked the question anyway. "What are you going to do?"

"Interesting question, Wilsonia. I'm going to kill him. Now that I know he's a weak bitch, he doesn't deserve that guitar. There's no way he's a real guitar player."

"Yeah, he needs to die. Let's do that tomorrow."

"That's a good idea, Wilson. WWJD?"

"What would Jesus do?"

"No, stupid. What would Johnny do? Johnny Cash. Johnny Cash would shoot the man just to watch him die."

"That'll teach 'em."

"Johnny Cash said he came up with that line because that's the worst reason a person could have for killing another person."

"Now you have two reasons."

"Unless something changes today, instead of killing him, I'll make his life miserable for a week or two so I can gather more material. That's what the pillow man would do."

"Let's eat some mushrooms," Wilson said. "You're killing my buzz."

<❁>

"What are you doing here?" Wilson's better half asked as her husband showed me a picture on his phone she would never see.

"Planning a murder," I answered in all honesty. "What's for dinner, Peggy?"

"Probably not turkey. Why do men always want to set things on fire?"

"Why do people drive on parkways and park on driveways?" And, with that, party pooper Peggy went back upstairs to ask herself when and where it all went wrong. Wilson went to see a man about a horse.

That's when Irma made the mistake of entering the sanctuary. "Did you lose a bet or was yours one of those arranged marriages?" I asked.

"That's not a very nice thing to say, Patrick."

"I don't trust people who say nice things."

"I don't trust Felix anymore. He's been hanging out at that sketchy bar down the street from our house. That shithole on Figueroa."

"Wow. That place is special. Have you been in there before, Irma?"

"God, no! It looks like they serve every kind of hepatitis in there."

"If it makes you feel any better, I guarantee you, Felix will never cheat on you with another woman."

"What the hell does that mean?"

"You'll figure it out. It took me a few months."

With the wife hi-how-are-yous out of the way, I asked my host, "Wilson, what's wrong with Felix?"

"He's alright, been acting a little weird lately. I've been so busy this year we almost never get to play golf on Fridays anymore."

"Irma says he's been hanging out at El Nuevo Paraiso."

Wilson's shock turned to sadness and then glee. "He's taking it in the ass at the tranny bar! Patrick, we're gathering so much material today!"

Shots of tequila and lines of Thanksgiving's finest marching powder weren't doing it, so, in an attempt to kill more brain cells, I asked Wilson, "What's your favorite Hendrix song?"

"Fire."

"Good one. Hendrix never asked for a refund. Not once. I like 'Crosstown Traffic' right now."

"You jump in front of my car, when ya—"

"Fun fact: 'Crosstown Traffic' had a different title in the UK."

"Different album cover, too. Have you ever fried a turkey?"

"Fuck no," I responded. "I've seen a lot of great videos of people doing that, though."

"Perfect, let's get this party started."

Wilson is that rare combination of a man who can read instructions, retain information, and follow directions. With thawed turkey submerged in hot oil, we retired to the lounge area for cocktails and conversation.

"Where did you meet a woman named 7-11?" Wilson rudely inquired.

7XI

"It's 'Cross Town Traffic' in the UK."

"I didn't ask about that, asshole," Wilson said.

"Her name is the number 7, the letter X, and the letter I," I explained.

"7XI?"

"Yeah. Awesome, huh?"

Wilson looked more confused than Felix's wife will be one day soon.

Outside the man cave on Wilson's big beautiful deck whose commanding view of the city below numbed most of the pain the drugs and alcohol neglected, the only object visible in the clear blue sky was the beautiful Southern California sunshine machine. "Turkey done in four more minutes!" Wilson announced with confidence as he read a thermometer or a timer or something like that.

Since Wilson had never heard this one before, I had to ask, "Have you seen my Tattoo?"

"No, I don't think so. I think I would remember that."

Down on one knee and in my best Hervé Villechaize accent I pointed at the sky and exclaimed, "The plane! The plane!" Wilson laughed harder than he should have and knocked over a bistro-height barstool-type chair setting off a chain of events we never discuss. The barstool slammed into the turkey fryer tipping it over; hot peanut oil slid off the side of the deck as it met the open flame beneath the turkey pot. A stream of nutty napalm ignited parched backyard brush on the hillside below in a loud poof. Wilson ran for a garden hose as I observed fire morph into a swirling vortex of flames best described as a fire tornado. Due to the favorable wind direction, the stiff breeze saved Wilson's home from certain destruction. Not everyone was grateful for that.

<✥>

Holidays are almost always a disaster for me. *Why me?* I asked myself as the Thanksgiving Mount Washington Fire Tornado roared down the hill behind Wilson's house gathering material as it carved a zig-zagging path of death and destruction through the hillside neighborhoods of Mount Washington and Highland Park before losing steam on the 110 freeway. Notable casualties of the inferno were the building formerly known as the Southwest Museum of the American Indian, the Self-Realization Fellowship International Headquarters, and the creepy little recreation center Black Patrick used to visit once a week for anonymous meetings. The ones for alcoholics, you weirdo. Anyway, the flaming twister's meandering route of terror also incinerated Mount Washington Elementary School, a supermarket, a taco stand, a taco truck, and at least 37 people.

As Peggy finished cooking the turkey in the oven, Wilson and I hid the turkey fryer, pressure-washed the deck, and removed all traces of fire damage. Plants, sod, and wood chips covered the scarred and charred earth, mission accomplished. Deep Purple's *Burn* provided the soundtrack.

"Where did that fire come from?" Felix asked.

"What fire?" I asked.

Wilson added, "We saw some fireworks earlier." Yes, we did. *Earlier* meaning July.

TWO

BLACK PATRICK FRIDAY

PASADENA

T HAT WARM FUZZY FEELING when you've survived another close call with a fire tornado. Hungover and expecting arson investigators to burst through the door of my apartment at any minute, a text message from Billthy Animal raised my spirits:

> I'm at Barney's Beanery

WeHo?

> Pasadena

On my way

In times of uncertainty, some turn to a higher power. Those misguided robots have never seen a fire tornado. Bill asked me the question I most feared: "How was your Thanksgiving?"

"I can't talk about it."

"You saw the fire tornado."

"What fire tornado?"

"The fire tornado you saw yesterday."

"What? I didn't start a fire tornado!"

"Try again. Pretend you're being interrogated by the cops," Bill advised as he launched into his creepy role-playing persona. "Tell me about the fire tornado, Mr. Patrick."

"I didn't see a fire tornado. I was with Bill at Barney's Beanery."

"You want me to believe you didn't see a fire tornado."

"Do you want me to lie? Listen, Uvalde, I know what I didn't see."

"Dude, do you really think insulting cops will help?"

"Of course it will. It always does. It's my civic duty. Insulting cops is essential and required behavior on my planet. Yours, too. Uvalde. The pig bastards have broken the social contract. We pay them to bravely, heroically, and courageously, help us when we need help. We don't pay them to be little bitches afraid of everything. Too scared to save a classroom full of 9-year-olds from a mass murderer. Over 370 of those cowards in costumes waited 77 minutes to confront the kid with the gun while he turned kids into Swiss cheese. Do you know why?"

Bill thought for a second and answered. "Because Billy Gibbons wasn't there to tell those pussies what to do."

"Exactly. Winner, winner, Barney's has a great fried chicken dinner."

<◈>

Once the beloved crew at Barney's completed shift change and our thorough analysis of the gravity-defying miracle of cosmetic surgery concluded, Bill and I got down to business.

"Why are you in Pasadena?" I asked Bill.

"I've been spending a lot of time here lately," Bill answered. "The other day I had a date with a woman here—"

Barney's Beanery Pasadena, California.

"A woman?"

"—things got interesting."

"How interesting?" I asked.

"We met for lunch. That woman can really put away the sausage if you know what I mean."

"Maybe—"

"We walked out of the Japanese restaurant and into the happy hour place—"

"Rocco's?"

"Exactly. Fire tornado. She kept eating. A pizza, an order of wings, it went on and on."

"Maybe she's bulimic."

"On the way out of happy hour, I tried to distract her, but she saw another restaurant and said, 'Buca di Beppo! My favorite!' so we went to dinner."

"Buca di Beppo has huge portions," I said because somebody said that once.

Despite all his rage, Bill confided, "I don't know if I'll ever see her again…"

"I'm sorry, Bill. Women like that don't grow on trees around here."

"They can't. She's at least 400 pounds. Anyway, I gave the server some money and got the hell out of there before I had to watch her eat again."

"Good move."

"Then I bought a record store. Let's go see it."

Bill parked in the back lot of Cranberry Records. "You've gotta be kidding me, Bill."

"You think it's a bad idea?"

"No! Everybody's been trying to buy this place forever. How did you do it?"

"It's a secret. Like your fire tornado. Cranberry is all mine January 2nd. I need you guys to help me update the place."

"No shit. I'll get Wilson over here right now."

The first thing Wilson said when he arrived at Cranberry was, "Sorry it took me so long. The fire department came by asking about a fire, for some reason. I told 'em I saw something that may have been a fire from a distance and somebody was lighting off fireworks earlier."

"From a distance! Felix tells his wife he appreciates the ladyboys from a distance. Negative two inches!"

"Funny, huh? The dumbass robot government-employee-slash-criminal was too stupid to ask a follow-up question."

"If a public servant solves a mystery he has to do more paperwork. Uvalde."

"Speaking of mysteries, I don't know what Peggy was talking to Irma about on the phone this morning but it sounded bad," Wilson said.

"How long do you think it'll be before Felix turns into Felicia?" I asked Wilson.

"Burnt," Bill said as he led us to the grand entrance of Cranberry Records. "Don't say anything until we're back in the car."

I said, "Anything," as soon as we walked into Cranberry Records. We may have been stoned. I can't remember.

Once the three of us completed our tour of Cranberry Records and were securely confined within his car, Bill asked, "What do you think?"

Wilson said, "I think I need a new calendar. What year is this? What kind of genius opens a retail store these days?"

Bill answered, "A fire tornado survivor."

What a dirty trick. That bastard bamboozled us into giving a shit about his ill-advised business venture. He must have known the few, the proud, the fire tornado survivors, would rally in support. Bill knew what we saw.

THREE

FELIX HAS A BUNKER

HIGHLAND PARK

T HE AIR WAS THICK WITH THE SMELL of cheap cleaning products, soiled adult diapers, and disappointment.

"What the hell was that?" I indignantly asked my drinking buddy.

Wilson responded immediately, "In some cultures shitting in an adult diaper while talking to a pre-op transsexual bartender is considered a sign of respect."

"Deference via defecation? It smells like death."

"You'll get used to it," Wilson said.

"What, exactly, did you and Felix do every Friday when you said you were doing golf things?"

"It was amazing, and I hope you understand."

"Don't tell me—"

"Felix is the only other man I know who truly appreciates a well-written and acted romantic comedy."

"I need rugs," a spirit animal within me said.

"Drugs?" Wilson asked.

"Rugs. The cold concrete floors in my cave loft are busting 7XI's knees open," I revealed. "I'm looking for rug burn, not impact wounds."

"I talked to your friend Bill about his record store plans earlier. He shared some new information."

"Awesome."

"Bill had another date with the woman who drove him to Cranberry that one night. He thinks she's good luck. Know what her name is?"

"No. Don't tell me—"

"7XL."

The sketchy bar on Figueroa Street.

El Nuevo Paraiso was one of those weird Mexican bars that salted the top of your beer bottle as a matter of course. I never figured out why. Wilson ended all confusion with a confusing statement: "Patrick, I have good news and bad news."

"Tell me the bad news."

"We will no longer do business outside of America after next year."

"Outstanding, there is a God. What's the good news?"

"We're going to Micronesia."

"Felix has a micro what?"

"Our last international client is an Australian billionaire in Micronesia."

"Phil Rudd?"

"Exactly. Whatever. I'll let you know when you need to know. Don't make any plans for February."

"Why? Did Felix qualify for the Olympics again, or something?" I asked.

An exasperated Wilson stared up at the popcorn ceiling festooned with dollar bills and peso notes upon which El Nuevo Paraiso's regulars wrote special messages to their favorites. Then a flood of tears streamed down his cheeks as a torrent of urine burst the banks of his diaper and soaked the thick carpet under his barstool. I took that as a signal to go outside and visit the man selling tacos under Christmas tree lights. Al pastor cures many ailments.

Cilantro and onion with lime juice always brings back memories. I remembered the days before I met Wilson. The long-lost days when I still had a glimmer of hope. People who asked questions asked Wilson and me, "What do you guys do, again?" again and again. Our employee handbook provided hundreds of canned responses to questions, all designed to obfuscate our secret mission. A complete list of those nuggets appears in the appendix to this work of art.

What did we do, again? Untold amounts of damage wherever we went. All while presiding over an empire.

Wilson founded EAD Logistics as a tax shelter, however, those plans backfired when business boomed in the wake of the Hacienda Heights Zombie Attack of 2017. As Wilson told the Los Angeles County Coroner in 2018, "HHZAXVII taught us all a hard lesson: be prepared. Make sure your recording studio is zombie-proof."

EAD Logistics tended to keep a low profile. We drove unmarked cars, eschewed the logo-embroidered polo shirts commonly worn by those in the logistics industry, and presented ourselves as recording studio specialists. Nobody needed to know we were building doomsday bunkers. And nobody needed to know EAD was an acronym for Eat a Dick.

"Why are we at Felix's tranny bar with you shitting in adult diapers?" I dared ask Wilson.

"The bowling alley guy finally bought this place and the properties next door on both sides. We're demolishing everything and going down."

"Like Freddie King."

"Like Felicia on the back nine. The bowling alley guy wants us to build an underground transsexual version of that mall in Singapore."

"Four floors of whores?"

"How do you know all of this stuff, Patrick?"

Indeed, EAD's next big thing would be an underground skyscraper. An amusement park concept I found highly amusing. "All I know is, one of the bars should be named Kickstands."

FOUR

GREAT LAKES, NO MISTAKES

MINNESOTA

M INNESOTA. Where cost-conscious bunker-building Americans too chickenshit to move to Alaska go.

"We're leasing a warehouse here," Wilson announced. "All the doomsday people say Minnesota is the place to be. Lots of lakes for drinking water, cool temperatures—"

"I met a woman from Minnesota in Los Angeles last week. She is a goddess living amongst us. Like a barely legal Peggy."

"She's too good for you, then."

"She asked me, no joke, 'Are there any lakes around here to go swimming in?'"

"What was your answer?"

"I informed the sweet young lady her magnetic resonance was elevating the atmospheric pressure creating a disturbance in my farm belt."

"Did she make your grain silo explode?"

"Almost. I launched my heat-seeking missile from its silo before that could happen."

"Did she go ballistic?"

"Nuclear."

Frequent visits to Minnesota's wastelands north of Minneapolis fed our bank accounts like no other. For the price of a shitty Barney's-adjacent condominium in any Los Angeles County neighborhood with a Beanery, one could own a hunting lodge on a hundred acres in Northern Minnesota. Most Minnesotans live in the Minneapolis-Saint Paul metropolitan area known as the Twin Cities. Those are the *cool* people. We did business with the real people.

Our first stop on the trek was to meet up with the superstar, miracle-working engineering and construction duo of Ed and Liz. Wilson met Ed when he sought to add a wine cellar and an outdoor living area with a kitchen plus bar in the backyard of his Palm Desert, California vacation home. The city and the homeowners' association approved plans for everything but the wine cellar.

Wilson interviewed every contractor in the Palm Desert area he could find. He collected estimates of construction costs while failing to find a courageous outlaw willing to build the wine cellar without permission. Until he met Ed, a young, quick, beast of a man living fearlessly on a higher spiritual plain. "Fuck those people," Ed said as Wilson told the tale of frightened contractors, uncooperative governmental bodies, and shitty nosy-neighbor organizations. "Give me copies of all your estimates right now. I'll match the lowest number and include the wine cellar for that price. I get shit done."

This guy's insane, Wilson said to himself. *What kind of drugs is he on? I'll have two of whatever he's having.* "Deal," Wilson said to Ed with a firm handshake as the two shared the kind of eye-to-eye contact warriors do before entering battle. "Fuck those people."

Most of the homes within Wilson's gated golf course community served as vacation rentals for Canadians escaping brutal winters, then sat empty the rest of the year. Wilson and Ed hatched a plan to subvert the oppressive laws and regulations assholes with nothing better to do enact and enforce in desert neighborhoods with golf courses.

Ed needed a 15-foot deep, 14-foot wide, 17-foot long hole in the ground to house a 12x15 wine cellar with 12-foot high ceilings. To eliminate any neighborhood complaints, Wilson reserved all of the vacation rental properties bordering his home for the week surrounding the Fourth of July holiday. Then he invited everybody in the neighborhood to a three-day party at the community clubhouse where live bands and DJs entertained at high volume for 12 hours every day and night. Wilson donated cases of beer and a pallet of explosive fireworks to local skater kids with instructions to launch the sky bombs at appointed times. Ed pre-positioned crew, heavy equipment, and construction supplies in the neighboring vacation rentals. At noon on the Fourth, one especially impressive, high-altitude, explosive flash-bang grenade stunned Palm Desert signaling, *GO!*

The concussive aerial blast stunned a driver delivering ice to the community center party, causing a head-on collision between the ice truck and a guy delivering a bouncy house.

Vehicular traffic in and out of Wilson's section of the neighborhood completely stopped. The wall separating the rear of Wilson's garage disappeared, heavy equipment entered the backyard and dug fast and deep. Excavators delivered soil to dump trucks in various directions across neighboring walls. In almost no time Ed had a giant hole in the backyard filled with preassembled concrete forms and steel reinforcement. Concrete trucks and pumps filled the forms as the floor and walls were poured quickly and simultaneously. With concrete poured, excavating equipment and all debris removed, the crew took a well-deserved break and retired to a vacation rental across the street to recharge and barbecue as concrete cured.

After a couple of hours, the crew returned, installed the concrete forms and steel reinforcement, then poured the roof of the wine cellar. Ed joined Wilson at the association clubhouse for a celebratory beverage. "We left thousands of pounds of ice and dry ice down there to keep the temperature under 500°," Ed told Wilson. "It's gonna get hot down there, keep the sand moist on top until we come back next week. The wall of your garage looks like it's always been there. The equipment's all gone, mission accomplished."

Wilson reported, "The tow truck driver dropped the ice truck on its side and it's still blocking the road."

"I wonder how that happened." expert secret mission planner Ed said.

"We're ready to pour the backyard patio slab next week?"

"Yes, as soon as we do that and the inspector leaves we install the missile silo entrance hatch to the wine cellar."

<⚑>

"The end, what a great story, Wilson. I have a feeling these farmers who want a connecting doomsday bunker are weirdos. They'd better not be horse people."

"Why? You haven't even met Olaf and Wilfred and you already know they're weirdos. Are you psychic?"

"No. All old people are kooks save for a very few lucky motherfuckers."

"Yeah? What makes an old fucker a non-kook in your fantasy world?"

"Wilson, you stupid fuck, there are only two ways to avoid being a stupid old fuck. One—die. Two—listen to Motörhead and Judas Priest."

I see the ghost of Lemmy Kilmister everywhere I go. Maybe because I want to. Probably because I need to. Lemmy didn't waste a minute of his life. Because he was rock 'n' roll from the moment he woke up until the moment he woke up again. I'm not explaining this to you, you either know or you will never know.

<②>

As we arrived at our first stop, a 9,000-square-foot bunker hidden under a shuttered hardware store on the side of a highway in Northwest Minnesota, the magnificent Ed was loading up his truck for the road trip to our next location. Ed toured the bunker for us as the spectacular Liz put the finishing touches on the underground palace (more on Liz later) Then we hit the road headed for an undisclosed location still mostly populated by Norwegians in denial that their ancestors arrived a long time before the fake historical figure known as Christopher Columbus did. I rode with Ed.

"What was the toughest part of the hardware store project?" I asked Ed.

"Having to tell the ladies from the reservation I'm gay."

"I don't even want to know."

"Word spread around the reservation about my massive hog," Ed disclosed. "The hotel bar filled with squaw."

"I've heard the ancient legend of the relentless, hog-hunting squaw—they're no joke."

"I had to ask the chief for help, it got so weird. The chief showed up and demanded to inspect my hog."

"No—"

"It was the only way out, Patrick. Every time I'm in Minnesota, the same thing, same old song and rain dance."

"Did you change your settings on Hinge?"

"I keep forgetting to do that."

Olaf and Wilfred shared a property boundary dividing their respective timberlands. Olaf's 320-acre forest to the north; Wilfred's 240-acre timber farm to the south. The town administration approved plans for a contemporary shipping container accessory dwelling unit on a portion of Olaf's property between his home and Wilfred's. A clever disguise for the doomsday bunker Ed and Liz would soon turn from back-of-napkin sketch to reality.

"Olaf nailed it at the town council meeting," Ed related:

> "I met this young man at a prayer breakfast in Sioux Falls last year. I asked Ed what his favorite bible passage was. Ed said, 'I am a carpenter.' Broke my heart. I know how difficult being a carpenter is these days. When I told Ed about my daughter, Winnie, and her dreams of writing her books about Jesus in a place amongst the trees, Ed said, 'I

am a carpenter.' By the time we finished our pancakes, I knew Ed was a carpenter. Just like Jesus."

"By the time Olaf finished the acid was kicking in. The town council members grew pelican heads and approved our plans unanimously. We drove back to Olaf's place dodging moose, deer, and air guitar players eating fire-breathing quesadilla dragon gods flying underneath scuba-diving horseshoes in the sky."

"Are you sure about that?" I asked Ed.

"I know what I saw."

"Where the hell did you get the acid?"

"Wilfred has a lab."

Wow. Just goes to show it's foolish to underestimate anybody anywhere. My presumption people in rural Minnesota were like rural people in parts of Ohio and Indiana—cousin fuckers—may not have been 100% accurate. Except for the parts of Minnesota near North Dakota where family trees have no branches.

We lost Wilson along the way to Olaf's farm, and Ed was concerned. Wilson was a big boy. I told Ed, "No big deal, Wilson has a phone."

"Patrick, you don't understand, there is no cell signal anywhere near here."

"You're telling me Norwegians don't have good cell phone reception? What are you gonna tell me next? New Yorkers don't know good pizza? That's crazy talk."

FIVE

MASTER OF THE PUPPETPLAN

PASADENA

B ACK IN LOS ANGELES, A THEY NAMED FELIX WAS UNHINGED. "Patrick, you can judge me 'til your face is blue."

"Felicia, what's your problem? I don't judge. And your face really is blue. Go back to Sephora and fix that shit."

"Yeah, you're right," Felix said. "These estrogen shots are —"

"Fucking with you subliminally. That's what happens."

"I guess so. It's like a weapon you can't see."

"A weapon? So, you still haven't had the operation?"

"Patrick, are you transphobic or just a total asshole? Your jokes are never funny."

"I wasn't joking. You might wanna take a step back and realize it's not all about you once in a while, Felicia."

"Right. I know. You try walking around with a target on your back every day."

"Motherfucker, the monkey on the target on my back has a target on his back. You think you know what it's like. You don't know what it's like. You don't know what it's like! You don't know shit."

Felix/Felicia outside his/her favorite bar.

"Have you ever worn a little black dress?" Felix asked.

"Fuck no. Where did you ever get the idea to wear a little black dress?"

"I was on the wrestling team in high school—"

"You can stop right there."

"I learned all the wrong holds; the coach suggested I switch from wrestling to volleyball. It worked. I got a scholarship to a subpar educational institution in a California cowtown."

"What was the most difficult part of playing volleyball in college?"

"Telling my parents I'm gay."

In an attempt to change the subject, I asked Felix/Felicia, "Did you know, one in six dogs can be classified as serious poop eaters?"

"My dog likes to smell it, but doesn't eat it."

"My friend, Bob, lives on a farm. His dog doesn't eat dog poop, but he loves horse poop."

"Bob or his dog?"

"Well, I won't speculate."

There's no problem electric guitars played loudly through gigantic stacks of amplification can't solve. Prove me wrong and I'll give you a dollar. 7XI was a very patient woman, for the most part.

"You told me you would teach me feedback meditation when you came back from Minnesota," 7XI said.

"I'm a big fat liar, Seven."

"You don't think I'm ready. I hate you!"

"Stop that. Have I ever asked you if you're ready?"

"No. You just do it."

"You'll know when you know I know you know you're ready."

Maybe Wilson was right. He was always telling me, "Wait until they're 19, 18 is too soon."

My question was and remains, "Why risk being too late?" Wilson never had a good answer for that.

SIX

LIVE AT THE ICE HOUSE

PASADENA

V ARIETY IS THE SPICE OF LIFE. And 7XI needed a break from her main squeeze, so I invited Peggy's sister, DD, to see funnyman Ron White at the Ice House.

"Is DD your real name?" I asked my date.

"No, they're fake."

It was as if DD'd never had a conversation with a man about a topic other than her tits. So I just went with it. We talked about her tits all night and well into the next morning. If there's a better conversation piece out there than DD's DDs I'd like to see the evidence.

"How was your date last night?" Wilson asked.

"God bless America," I responded.

"What was the highlight?"

"The peanut oil. The peanut oil smoked but didn't catch fire and kill all the puppies in an animal hospital, this time."

"It's genetic," Wilson said. "Irma told Peggy she found ladies' underwear in Felix's glove compartment. She thinks Felix is cheating on her."

"Pay for Irma's private investigator and make sure we get a copy of all the footage."

DD & her DDs. You're welcome, Ron White.

"Do you really want to see that?"

"Of course! If my wife hired somebody to follow me around and film it we would laugh hysterically watching the footage the rest of our lives. Felix is a bro, whatever he wants to do is awesome and I support it. The crazier the better."

"Don't you think he's struggling through an existential crisis of some kind right now?"

"Yes! We all are! Any motherfucker with a pulse and a soul is struggling right now. Maybe Felix's miniskirt/crotchless panties coping mechanism is on another level, but whatever. It's not against the law."

"How many times a week do you use that line?"

"Which one?"

"It's not against the law."

"Are we including Braille and American Sign Language?"

"Sure."

"You know I volunteer at Guide Dogs for the Blind, right?"

"I do now."

"Have you ever seen a hot Filipina traveling nurse signing angrily at Black Patrick while topless at a Hooters?"

"Yes, of course. Surgically enhanced small D/large C pierced nipples."

"Costa Mesa?"

"You must be psychic."

<&>

The rest of the company meeting at Barney's Beanery consisted of the typical, "How the fuck are we gonna get away with that?" questions endemic to massive construction projects executed in complete secrecy. One might presume rural areas far away from civilization offer a respite from the uniformed gangs in cute little costumes Americans love so much. Au contraire, mi amor, the countryside is crawling with scads of fish and wildlife officers, forestry department flunkies, dumbass county sheriffs deputies, stupid state troopers, federal land management pinheads, and even more tax takers eager to justify their positions. Not to mention every asshole who isn't a cop is a wannabe cop and thinks they're a cop entitled to be all up in your business. Since we can't kill people or blow up bridges to keep the bastards away, we employ creative diversionary tactics when necessary. You might be surprised how easy it is to fake a UFO landing or Bigfoot sighting, for example.

Speaking of UFOs, Bill showed up and wanted to talk about his new record store.

Bill told us, "San Clemente is one mid-sized earthquake or fire tornado away from oblivion."

"That's not good," I said.

"Yeah, that town has a lot of character," Bill said.

"No, it doesn't," I countered. "San Clemente has a whole lot of nothing. If San Clemente goes away the people who survive spread out and pollute the rest of the planet."

Bill wasn't angry. "Patrick, you need a puppy."

Bill informed us he wanted to start Honker Records Pasadena with a completely clean slate, meaning all display fixtures, equipment, and inventory in stock would go away.

"Great idea, Bill," Wilson said. "That's easier for us."

Bill had a bottom-feeding eBay seller lined up to remove all of the existing inventory and display fixtures starting at 12:01 a.m. on January 2nd. At 5 a.m. 1-800-GOT-JUNK would make quick work of whatever crap remained. The arrival of Ed, Liz, electricians, plumbers, and laborers at 7 a.m. would kick off the transformation of the building and the birth of the greatest record store in Pasadena history. Motherfucker.

Then Bill told us he didn't have any money to pay for anything.

"When were you going to tell us about that?" Wilson asked Bill.

"I wasn't planning anything. I figured you guys could handle that part."

Bill was right. We handled it and took an equity stake in a business nobody in their right mind would ever invest in.

7XI was raised by wolves in a hippie commune, as far as I could tell. She followed the Grateful Dead around for most of her childhood then became a gutter punk. Thank God she started shaving at some point.

"7XI, you mean everything to me."

"Aww, thank you, Black Patrick," 7XI responded. "You're really nice sometimes. Most old guys get mean when I tell them they're old guys."

"Those old guys are what professionals like me refer to as old cunts."

"How do you know I'm not the cunt?"

"If you cunt figure it out, I cunt tell you how to figure it out."

"I cunt rely on you, anymore? I cunt be with a man I cunt count on."

"You cunt."

'I cunt what?"

"I was simply calling you a cunt."

SEVEN

HELLO?
HELLO!
HELLO.

MAINE | NEW YORK | TORONTO

F INAL ROAD TRIP OF THE YEAR FOR EAD. "Are you coming over for Christmas?" Wilson asked. "DD will be there."

"No way. I'm leaving the country and forgetting everything I know about holiday occasions at your house."

"Peggy will be bummed," Wilson said. "Where are you going?"

"Cambodia."

"A holiday in Cambodia?"

"Yes. There is no winter in Cambodia. It's, like, 80° there in December. We spend way too much time in cold places."

"That's because smart people are planning to bunker down in those cold places. "

"Should we tell 'em it doesn't matter? That six extra months of life without the internet isn't worth it?"

"I'll be trapped with Peggy and DD."

"When we get back to Los Angeles we need to convince Bill 7XL is the one."

"No. Absolutely not. We stopped doing conspiracies, remember?"

"No. What do Peggy and DD talk about?"

"Tits."

"Anything else?"

"No. It's fun watching movies with DD. If there aren't any tits she complains about the lack of tits."

After quick calculations, I deduced, "What you are saying is, DD is a 15-year-old boy."

"You call your girlfriend Seven."

"Let's talk about tits."

<&>

"Liz is meeting us in Buffalo," Wilson said as we descended into the airport in Maine.

"Fuck yeah, Liz is the best."

"After Maine, we're nailing down the Lockport deal then taking Liz to Toronto for her birthday."

"Beautiful. Are we taking care of Ed and Liz? I've never seen two people deliver the goods like those two. They're like Glenn Tipton and K.K. Downing."

"No. Those fuckers kill themselves working miracles, man," Wilson said. "Two months of vacation is not enough. We want them healthy and happy for a long, long time."

"What's the plan?"

"After Liz's birthday party, you're flying to Minnesota to see Ed. While you're telling Ed he gets another month of paid vacation every year I'm telling Liz the same thing."

"Awesome."

"The plan is they go three months on, one month off. We plan around their time off. We can do it that way, that means we do it that way." Wilson continued, "We can't grow the company by expecting those guys to work harder and harder. Humans wear out. We need 'em to look out for the next Ed and Liz and we grab it when they see it. We can't go looking for that, the stars align and deliver the goods if and when it happens."

"Only after Rob Halford makes a special sound announcing goods are to be delivered. When did you get so spiritual, Wilson?"

"When Peggy went out of town and DD came over. DD's nipples are pierced now."

"There is a God—"

"I swear I saw electrical currents connecting all kinds of things that weekend."

"So that's why your phone was on Do Not Disturb..."

"She was delivering the goods. I reciprocated. Together we worked our way from *Killing Machine* to *Screaming for Vengeance*."

"I don't understand people who think *Point of Entry* is a weak Priest record. 'Heading out to the Highway' and 'Don't Go' are amazing songs."

Wilson looked at me like I was crazy and said, "I wanna go—"

"You wanna go hot rockin.'"

"I still can't believe how great *Unleashed in the East* is."

"I can. Notice how the title doesn't say anything about the record being a live album. All of those live records from the 1970s are fake."

"What about *Double Live Gonzo*?"

"Please, we're supposed to believe Ted's record company paid to record his shitty live shows for 18 months and the best shit happened in San Antonio and Nashville? Those towns didn't care about that guy."

"I've never been able to figure out why none of the songs from *Free for All* were on the live record."

"Meat Loaf sang lead vocals on most of *Free for All*."

"What?"

"Wilson, everything we think we know, we don't know. Whatever we believe, we don't know. There are things we know and things we don't know."

"Listen, motherfucker," Wilson said as the guy on acid in the car with him forced him to use more brainpower than he wanted to, "we're stopping at the next Waffle House."

From the start, Wilson and I decided we didn't want to have a company unless our company was the best fucking company on Earth to work for. Why do it any other way? Any other way means you're not taking care of your people. Ed and Liz make more money than we do. They're more important than we are. They know that. We give them all the tools they need to succeed. Sometimes they fuck up. So? They're human. We all fuck up sometimes. We talk about it, fix it, laugh about it, and get back to business. Ours is not a punishing world. Maybe that's why we make so much fucking money. Try it sometime.

EIGHT

HOLIDAY IN CAMBODIA

HO CHI MHIN | ANGKOR WAT

W HAT A RELIEF. The 20 hours on the Japan Airlines 787 Dreamliner from Los Angeles to Ho Chi Minh City cleansed my brain of all things America. Except for the American airplane I was on. Those Boeing 787 Dreamliners are magical airplanes with hidden, miraculous superpowers I am inclined to believe are beyond the ability of humans to detect with the five senses included at birth. Behind the scenes, below-the-line creatures operate mysterious devices and perform kung fu operations required to deliver essential vitamins and minerals we will never know about. Like infrared light, we don't see it, but it's there making all the difference.

I asked Billthy Animal where to stay in Ho Chi Minh City and he told me, "The only place to stay in HCM is Japan

Town." Done. I'm there. That bastard didn't tell me Japan Town was wall-to-wall Vietnamese hookers. If that's what I was looking for I could have stayed at the Motel 6 in Westminster. Two nights in Vietnam were enough, time to fly to Siem Reap, Cambodia.

How many people still believe every giant building from a leftover civilization is a temple built to worship some implausible bullshit? All of those pyramids in Egypt are monuments to pharaohs? The pyramids in the Yucatan were constructed for religious ceremonies? I'm sorry to burst your bubble—people had better shit to do than worship their gods and have goofy ritualistic ceremonies all day every day. Like grow food, generate electricity, power spaceships—the list goes on and on. All the shit we find buried in the desert is not left behind by previous civilizations because the people who suddenly died in a mudflood were busy worshipping monkey gods or sacrificing virgins. By the way, has anybody ever wondered if the virgins sacrificed were killed because they were virgins because they were simply unattractive?

Angkor, in present-day Cambodia, was a happenin' place until a bunch of Thai people showed up on fighting elephants, stole the king's harem of 3,000 hot Thai women, and enslaved everybody they didn't kill. After that, nobody went anywhere near the place. Some people hung out around on the fringes, ever afraid the fighting elephants would return, one would presume, so they never went back inside the temple, that's for sure. Or so we are led to believe.

In 1860 a French naturalist hacked his way through the Cambodian jungle in search of exotic insects. Instead, he found Angkor Wat. After that, Henri Mouhot was found by an exotic insect that bit him and killed him.

Henri asked around town before he got what he deserved. The locals told him the city had always been there or was built in one night by Gods, or, my favorite, it built itself.

Modern-day archaeologists, i.e. incredibly unimaginative people paid to slowly, and I mean slowly, dig shit up with paint brushes and tell us what the government wants us to hear, believe the entire enormous city was built by people who quarried and transported giant rocks on bamboo rafts from 20 miles away. Then elephants helped them with the rest.

Let me be the first to tell you—you're fucking stupid if you believe any of that bullshit. Never talk to anybody for the rest of your life. Don't have kids. You have failed every intelligence test, Neil deGrasse Tyson. An ancient civilization of super-intelligent people or some other creatures built that shit. You can't tell me with a straight face that shit was built by people like the losers we interact with all day every day. I'm sorry, I know your 401(k) is doing great and your golf score is improving year after year, but that doesn't mean you're not a dumbfuck, Wilson.

Are we really supposed to believe the most insanely beautiful and well-constructed building on the planet was built less than a thousand years ago and all the people who lived near there forgot about it for hundreds of years? There's no fucking way. Built by incredibly artistic slaves with fantastic technical and engineering skills? It didn't happen that way. And it's unlikely to be a temple of any kind. It was probably a goddamned power plant.

PART 2
BUZINESS

NINE

HONKER RECORDS

PASADENA

HAPPY NEW YEAR! The party started on January 2nd at Bill's remarkable new record store location on Colorado Boulevard in Pasadena, California. The leftover Cranberry Records merchandise went to a bottom-feeding eBay seller. We bought a few pizzas with that cash. Everything else in the building left town forever in a dumpster. Floors, walls, ceilings, windows, and doors disappeared, giving Liz and Ed the blank canvas they needed to fuck Pasadena up. Ed and Liz beautified Honker Records and set Bill up for guaranteed success then left town to knock out Maine and New York.

Fixtures from Bill's neighbor's cabinet shop in San Clemente arrived followed by merchandise, electronics, and artwork. Bill, former Cranberry employee Robbo, and a new cast of characters opened Honker Records quietly in late January to immediate success.

The first day we were in the space, Bill said, "I think the basement's pretty big." We were so busy clearing out 70 years' worth of wreckage from the sales floor that Bill's information didn't register. A few days later, over a celebratory end-of-day pile of cocaine, Bill said the same thing and took me downstairs.

Bill and Black Patrick outside Honker Records.

"What the fuck?" I exclaimed as Bill hit the lights. Although the space was piled high with decades of detritus, the room was nothing short of epic. I called 1-800-GOT-JUNK and we joined our brother at Barney's Beanery to strategize.

"Wilson, Bill's basement is larger than the footprint of his store and has 12-foot high ceilings," I said in a most casual manner.

Wilson was busy watching women's tennis, so I didn't think he noticed what I said. He looked at Bill and said, "Motherfucker, you have a 7,000-square-foot basement?"

"Yes, cocksucker, I do."

After drinks and drugs and dinner and drugs and drinks, we traveled to Honker Records. The last 1-800-GOT-JUNK truck was leaving as we arrived. The sight we beheld in the basement left all three of us speechless.

"What the fuck are we gonna do with this?" Wilson asked.

Bill had been thinking about the space all week. "We're gonna fill it with pussy."

In times of doubt, Wilson and I tended to retreat to our safe place—Barney's Beanery. This time we elected to hold our board of directors' meeting in the basement of Barney's.

"Nothing, and I mean nothing, we can possibly do with all of that basement space will ever generate revenue, let alone turn a profit," I told Wilson.

"No shit. We'll need to install a goddamn elevator and do all kinds of stupid shit to get that space permitted."

"What about pickleball?" I asked Wilson just to piss him off.

"Excellent idea, Maybe I'll move in there and sell my house," Wilson said.

TEN

OCEANIA UBER ALLES

AUSTRALIA - MICRONESIA

SOMETIMES I THINK WILSON AND I SHOULD TAKE SEPARATE FLIGHTS. "How was your vacation to Cambodia?" Wilson asked.

"History is a set of lies agreed upon," I replied.

International travel was always a gamble for Wilson and I. Narrow escapes from third-world countries appear more enjoyable on television than they are in reality. Since we needed the business, Wilson agreed to meet with a friend of a golf buddy in Melbourne, Australia to discuss a job on an undisclosed island. Something smelled bad. Either Felix/Felicia was behind some kind of medical tourism scam or Wilson needed to do a solid for the mob to cover gambling debts. *What's the worst thing that can happen?* I asked myself.

"The creepy motherfucker who bought the Hendrix Strat just sent me another text message."

I'm okay with the back plate, already ordered correct trem, I'll eat both of those, but your original listing stated it had the original pickups, which it does not. Since you purchased it new from Sweetwater and they do a 55 point inspection on all guitars, not sure how the pickups got swapped but they aren't correct and decreases the value, but more importantly those are the pickups that I was buying when I purchased the guitar. if you can find a full of the originals we could swap and I'll give you the pups that are in it now. I searched eBay and the cheapest full set I could find was $139 plus tax ($13), so $153 total for the pups. That's why I suggested a cash refund of $100. I'll eat the $50 loss on that and it would be quicker and easier for both of us. I do love the guitar and would like to keep it, but if it's not what I paid for then as a last resort I would like to return it for a full refund, my 1st choice is a refund of $100 via PayPal or Zelle, or provide me with the correct pickups and we'll swap the ones in there now for the correct ones.
Per your listing:

ELECTRONICS
Neck Pickup Pure Vintage '65 Gray-Bottom Single-Coil
Middle Pickup Pure Vintage '65 Gray-Bottom Single-Coil
Bridge Pickup Pure Vintage '65 Gray-Bottom Single-Coil
Either way, please advise, thank you!

"Aw, man. How did we forget to kill that guy?" Wilson wondered aloud, alerting the obvious yet undercover federal air marshals on the plane in the row in front of us. "I hate that guy more than anyone and I've never even met him."

"I sold the loser a $1,200 guitar for $600, he took it all apart and says some of the parts are not original. I bought the guitar new from Blackwater, opened the box, and played it a few times. The stupid cunt is wasting my time asking for a $100 refund. There's a special place in hell's butt rape room for little bitches like that motherfucker. He must have been bullied mercilessly as a kid."

Wilson read the text and said, "What a cunt. We need to turn this plane around a murder that guy right now."

"We decided to let him live for the free entertainment, remember?" I reminded Wilson.

"It's not funny anymore."

"And you were busy landscaping your hill."

"That's right. We were still covering up the—ow! What was that elbow for?"

For the rest of the flight to Melbourne, Wilson and I pretended to write a screenplay about crazy music business people covering up murders of Craigslist scammers. Why were we heading to Melbourne, Australia, you ask, again? Because a Micronesian billionaire insisted we party with him there for a couple of days. I asked my traveling partner a serious question before arrival in Melbourne: "Wilson J. Wilson, why are you always selected for secondary cavity search upon arrival in Australia?"

"Motherfucker! If you fucking sent an anonymous tip again I will kill you." That did it, the air marshals led Wilson to the VIP room where intimacy is not only encouraged, it is expected.

Wilson emerged from the bizarre government-sanctioned butt-fingering department with tousled hair and a half-untucked shirt. "They're waiting for you in Micronesia, asshole."

"Are those new shoes?"

"No. I've had these for years. Why do you ask?"

"You squeak when you walk."

"The Australians are using a new lube for the cavity searches. It smells like kangaroo and tastes like eucalyptus."

"Wilson, you're not supposed to taste the glove."

"It wasn't the glove."

ELEVEN

A FEW (DOZEN) RESENTMENTS

COOKIN' FROM THE INSIDE OUT

W HILE WILSON WAS ON HIS FIRST DATE WITH THE HOLE-SEARCHING CUSTOMS OFFICIALS, I had a flashback to an unhappy time in my life sullied by comminations with an equally sadistic type of subhuman.

You never know what's happening inside the mind of a sick fuck. One day I made the mistake of conversing with a truly demented and disturbed man. Without provocation, the emotionally stunted and friendless creep let loose a tirade of baby talk befitting a toddler. Pent-up anger and festering misery eating the smarmy old cocksucker alive—resentments —flew from his mouth like projectile dung from the rear of a bull with diarrhea. The ferocity of the shitstream made me wonder if the beast had been gang raped by an offensive line at some point in his formative years. I don't think that is the case—it was probably the entire football team and maybe even the coaching staff. Afterward, he may have been told, "IT'S YOUR *FAULT!*" as he walked awkwardly and with a limp out the doors of that steamy locker room. The team may have gone as far as to tell the recently-deflowered young man, "GET A *JOB!*" for good measure. Sound advice, if you ask me.

I spoke with my spiritual adviser after the unfortunate encounter with said lunatic. Guru PopesterJ (GPJ) wasn't as convinced people who kick people when they are down are all raping babies or murdering cheerleaders, but he didn't rule it out. "That man is very sick and insecure, Black Patrick. He lacks the tools to communicate with humans. Stay far away from that spiritual black hole," GPJ said. He then related a prescient anecdote from his own life. "I prayed for [name redacted] to die and it worked." Wow! I'm not doing that. I did do something similar to that for a few weeks when a certain weak bitch was elected to a political office. My prayers at the Devil's Gate Dam portal to hell remain unanswered by Satan. I didn't include an expiration date, so there is hope for the itinerant politico and his entire family of criminal cunts to perish. The sooner the better, Satan.

Although I am far from a religious man, excluding my devout worship at the electric church of rock 'n' roll, prayer works very well for me when faced with unreasonable and abusive dumbfuck losers. Here's how I rid my body and soul of resentments before memories of the shitheads eat me alive:

Every day for two weeks I say the following prayer:

"Dear God in Heaven, if it be your holy will, look with favor upon the health, happiness, and prosperity of [name of the asshole/group/organization you really should resent, but you're better than that] I ask You this in the Name of Jesus, the Lord."

Feel free to insert the name of whatever deity or former Motörhead member you choose. It almost doesn't matter what words you say, just do it.

I don't know how the resentment prayer works and it doesn't matter. It simply works. At times, I have had a list as long as 34 assholes to pray for. An asshole can ruin your whole day, but, after two weeks of prayer for that motherfucker, a feeling of peaceful forgiveness will replace visions of RPGs and homemade napalm. The sniper rifle returns to the gun safe and you are free to experience the joy of televised team sports once again. Like a champion.

TWELVE

WELCOME TO TAZMANIA

BRING IT

MICRONESIA'S MOST FAMOUS WEIRDO, TAZ, was waiting for us outside of customs. "Bloody 'ell! What took you so long?"

"Wilson always hides a little bit of cocaine in his asshole," I said, "so he gets a thorough prostate massage in every country."

"Which country is the best for that?" Taz asked.

Wilson replied, "In Estonia, there's a lineup of customs officers and a menu of services to choose from."

"Wow, how far away is that from here?" I asked.

"We'll find out," Wilson answered. "In Vietnam, a woman takes you into a room, gets naked, performs a sword swallowing show, and does that nuru massage thing before the surprise fist attack."

Digging for information, Taz asked. "What's the worst?"

"Portland. Sometimes big hairy women set up a bootleg checkpoint outside of Portland and pose as officers of s fake native American tribe so they can fist people."

"That sounds like a lot of work."

An eager-to-please Wilson elaborated, "Yes, it really does sound like they're working their fists up in there really hard. Somebody told me they only select people they suspect to have unusually tight sphincters for internal inspections. Some fake officers go elbow deep 15 times a day."

Redirecting the conversation to business, I said, "I wonder if any of them know how to work with concrete."

"I asked last time," Wilson said. "One was a bricklayer and one was a finish contractor."

"No plumbers?"

<☉>

Whilst restaurant and bar hopping in Fidler's Lane we learned Taz was a billionaire because he owned half the brothels in Melbourne. And every waitress in Melbourne is a sex worker. Wilson told Taz he wanted to go to a jazz club, so we did that. I told Taz I wanted to go to Nagambie.

"Are you mental, mate?"

"Yes, of course I am. I want to go to Nagambie Speedway," I told our host.

"Alright. I own a winery in Nagambie. Very well."

On the road to the airport where Taz kept one of his planes, he said, "Everybody who comes to Melbourne comes here for the hookers. What's the matter?"

Wilson lied and said, "My wife and her sister can't get enough of this."

I lied, too, and said, "7XI has worn me out."

"You own a 7-11? I own the Gold Coast 7-11 franchise."

"Where's that?"

"Queensland!"

How Taz snuck a raccoon into kangaroo land is a mystery.
Perhaps he hid it under his hat.

I let Wilson take over the conversation from there. Taz flew us to Nagambie where we were whisked off to his winery estate. Over a lamb roast and a few bottles of Taz's killer shiraz, Taz asked, "Why the hell do you want to go to Nagambie Speedway? Ten thousand visitors, never once has anyone asked to visit Nagambie Speedway."

Wilson answered, "Patrick's a big Tropical Fuck Storm fan."

"Fuck me," Taz said, "I know those wankers. You should have told me."

"Sorry. We're just dummies building bunkers pretending we're building recording studios."

"Do you build recording studios?"

Wilson said, "Yes, we've built more than 20."

"Interesting…" Taz said as I waited for the bomb blast. "I want you to build me a recording studio in the hotel I just bought. We'll go there tomorrow."

I am slow, at my best. Most times my brain works in reverse. So it took me until breakfast the next morning to realize and relay the following critical information to Wilson. "Hey, Wilson. The drummer in Tropical Fuck Storm does construction work."

"So?"

"The band's on hiatus. Let's find her and send her to Maine to work with Ed and Liz. We're gonna need somebody here and in Pohnpei."

"Okay. Is that why we're in Nagambie? Did you plan this?"

"Wilson, God laughs at people who make plans. I don't know anything about her, I don't even know her name. I can tell she's a badass construction superstar who can do what we do."

"Get shit done?"

"Get shit done."

Tropical Fuck Storm's drummer showed up just as the Maine project was wrapping up. The gang set off for Lockport, New

York for the next chapter. Liz and Ed called Wilson and me one day and Liz said, "Hammer does the work of five people, she's smarter than all of us combined, and she's fucking fun. We're never letting her go."

"Who's Hammer?" I asked.

"Lauren, dummy. That's her nickname."

"Who's Lauren?"

"Ed, you talk to these dumbfucks."

"Lauren is the drummer's name. Hammer is her nickname. I don't know how you found her."

"YouTube. I just knew she was a great drummer."

Once you've been around for a while and hired and fired thousands of people, you've seen the movie before. You know how it starts, the middle is what it is, and the ending is predictable. Assholes are easily detected. Losers are apparent. Superstars are difficult to locate in the wild, so I use YouTube. Pro tip. You're welcome. The first one's free.

By the time Wilson, Taz, and I arrived in Pohnpei, Micronesia we were all near death. Why Wilson felt the need to ask Taz if he knew anybody who owned a distillery or where to get uncut Peruvian cocaine remains a mystery to me to this day. Micronesia was no picnic, either, after New South Wales, let me tell you. The cocaine did help, however.

"Pay attention, ladies," Taz said as he roared away from the airport in Pohnpei's only vintage Land Cruiser. "This is the port where containers arrive on occasion." A couple of minutes later we were in the rear of a hardware store, "My business partner in the hotel owns this place. We can drop containers here and leave 'em here as long as we want if we need to."

A lap around the hardware store sent us up a dirt road, "This is the private road to my home. Exactly one kilometer to paradise." Taz showed us what we had already seen from space, our mission was clear.

"Have you ever dug up a swimming pool to put in a doomsday bunker?" Taz asked.

Wilson replied, "Yes, but it wasn't the only swimming pool on the island."

"It's the only swimming pool for a thousand kilometers, mate. What do you think about digging out the pool and going lower with the bunker, then adding the pool back on top."

"That's what I would do," I said because it was the worst idea in the world.

"Done. Let's do it," Taz decided. "We're off to Nan Madol tomorrow, lads. Maid service arrives in your rooms at the crack of dawn."

"Where do you find all of these waitresses?" Wilson asked.

"Do you want me to tell him?" I asked Taz.

After the awakening by talented members of Taz Mania Hotel's maid service, Wilson, Taz, and I boarded the SS *Tazamataz* for the voyage to Nan Madol.

"Thanks for the maid service, Taz," Wilson said.

"Maid service? Those were hookers, stupid. Are there schools in America?"

"Not really," I told Taz. "American schools are holding cells for kids not quite ready for prison. Does Pohnpei have a jail?"

"No," Taz responded. "We all know each other here, we have schools, there aren't a bunch of assholes here locking people up in cages for shits and giggles. Your American cops wouldn't last an hour on Pohnpei."

"Is that why Micronesia severed ties with the United States?" I asked.

Taz answered, "One reason. Another reason is Americans are really fucking stupid."

"We have sports in schools," Wilson said.

"That's fucking stupid. Why not have school in schools? Sports in schools. Think about it. Any objective view of that concept would lead Einstein, Hawking, and Kaczynski to the same conclusion."

Wilson looked at me and said, "Don't say it—"

"Neil deGrasse Tyson is a bitch."

Our tour of Pohnpei led us out the shipping channel past the airport and in a clockwise direction around the island. First stop—a beachfront bakery for breakfast. Fortified with a nutritional boost we powered on to our magical destination. "We have a meeting with the chief," Taz said.

"Cool."

"He's more like a king. Have you ever met royalty?" Taz asked.

"No," Wilson and I both said.

"I have," Taz said. "Those inbred Brits are strange. The chief is not like that. He is a wise and powerful man who deserves our respect. Please be kind."

"No problem."

"The chief will allow us access to his kingdom based on his perception of your value as a human being," Taz said.

"It's a good thing we didn't bring Neil."

It's good to be the chief. Taz brought sushi, fresh fruit, chocolate, and fine whiskey as tribute, the chief reminded me of any big fat guy in an aloha shirt. Once Taz explained who Wilson and I were, the chief wanted to know more.

"Nothing in Nan Madol is like anything else in Nan Madol. Nothing in Nan Madol is like anything else in Pohnpei. Nothing in Pohnpei is like anything else in the world. This is a special place, blessed by Gods, cursed by demons, haunted by ghosts, littered with the bones of unwelcome visitors. A land of many questions, and no answers. Why are you here, Wilson?"

"I am a spiritual man. I seek knowledge and wisdom," Wilson said. The chief rolled his eyes and looked at Taz like he wanted to kill him.

"What about you, Black Patrick?"

I told the aloha shirt guy, in all honesty, "I want to sit in silence on your sacred grounds and listen to the wind blow, taste the air, breathe the same oxygen your ancestors did, feel the magnetic vibrations of the basalt, absorb."

"What are you here on Pohnpei to do with my friend Taz."

"We're building him a recording studio," Wilson said.

"You will build your recording studio here, in Nan Madol," the chief told Taz.

"As you wish, chief," Taz said. "I shall return in 12 days to receive further instructions."

"Excellent, go see the tomb today."

"Holy shit, that was weird," I said to Taz.

"No shit. I've never been allowed anywhere near the tomb before," Taz said. "That's the most cursed spot here. Tell Fiona in Melbourne she was always my favorite."

"Where did they find this chief guy?" Wilson asked Taz.

"It's a bloodline deal. The chief's dad was the chief before him. The chief always goes away as a young man, learns worldly things, then returns to reign over the 27 people who live in Nan Madol with some knowledge of the outside world so he is not leading in a vacuum."

"Wow, that's interesting," I said. "What did the chief do in his time away from Nan Madol?"

"He went to Guam and got a job as a bus driver."

Taz was in shock after we met with the chief. That didn't stop him from guiding our tour of Nan Madol like a champion.

"The walls are built like log cabins out of basalt columns. The lightest columns weigh five tons. Historians believe the people who built Nan Madol floated the basalt logs here on bamboo rafts." This whole Nan Madol deal was beginning to sound a lot like my Christmas.

"What kind of bamboo was that?" Wilson asked.

"Exactly. There's no fucking way. Population 20,000 people, half are women, and half of that half are kids or old people, we're supposed to believe the entire male population of working age spent 300 years moving basalt around. About 800-ish years ago."

"I'll be the first to tell you," I said. "That didn't happen." And then I asked Taz, "What do you think happened?"

"All of this shit is more than 500,000 years old. It's the remnants of a power station on the continent of Mu. Sorcerers ten feet tall used acoustic resonance to levitate the basalt columns into place. What we see today is an elevated power plant that utilized the electromagnetic properties of basalt to repel typhoons. Beneath the sea lies an enormous capital city where unbelievably wealthy and prosperous, highly-advanced people, partied until the Earth's magnetic pole shifted in an instant sending a mile-high wall of water cruising around the planet for a few years."

I was inclined to agree, but couldn't help myself. "I wonder if the women here were hot?"

As goofy and haphazard as Wilson and I appeared to the outside world, our doomsday bunkers were engineered and constructed using the finest materials and with extreme attention to detail. With an average size of 10,000 square feet, our bunkers typically cost at least $15 million. That's $1,500 per square foot. It costs at least $500 per square foot to build a decent home in Los Angeles these days.

On the way out of Pohnpei, we met with Taz and gave him the good news. All three of the facilities we were building for him—the doomsday bunker on Pohnpei and the recording studios in Nagambie and Nan Madol—could be constructed using the same floor plan, reducing engineering and architecture expenses. Therefore, the total for all three would amount to $69 million. Taz wired the funds from the breakfast table, we were in business.

Cash in hand we placed massive materials orders with our suppliers of superstrong compounds. We never used metal in our reinforced concrete walls, floors, ceilings, tunnels, or staircases. Basalt rebar and mesh are stronger, lighter, and never rust. All of our cementitious materials were sourced from a mad scientist whose creations cured quickly and stronger than anything humans ever invented. We shipped all of our aggregate—crushed rock and sand— and concrete additives from our trusted suppliers to the job site. Concrete forms designed to our exact specifications arrived with all of the materials. There was never a single instance where a trip to a local hardware store was necessary.

Our approach was always to send twice as much material to a job site as we needed, in case something got lost in transit. So we promptly spent $12 million on materials, equipment, and shipping, and then asked ourselves if we were insane.

THIRTEEN

THE GRANDEST OF OPENINGS

PASADENA

S EVEN WEEKS OF THE HONKER RECORDS MACHINE FLYING AT SUPERSONIC SPEEDS using terrain-following radar to skim the surface of the earth without slamming into the side of Wilson's house led up to this very moment—the Honker Records Grand Opening Celebration. Bill farmed every contact in the record geek universe to create a frenzy of excitement and teased the record-collecting world with hints of the incredible items in stock dead people had left behind. A different live band performed every day for two weeks. A couple of superstar recording artists appeared for autograph signings announced at the last minute. A few times a day Bill saw a customer buying a record and said, "If you like that, you need this," and gave away a record he decided they needed, making a friend and gaining a customer for life. Bill eschewed cheesy advertising and marketing techniques in favor of dark humor in inappropriate places. Death metal records advertised in magazines for seniors, for example. Bill hired a troupe of clowns to march up and down Colorado Boulevard in Old Town Pasadena carrying picket signs protesting false metal. Bill created a stir within the Grateful Dead fan subculture when he announced the only three things he would never sell at Honker Records were Hitler's *Mein Kampf,* releases from The Offspring, and all Grateful Dead-related merchandise. Nobody cared about The Offspring.

Bill cajoled 7XI into working part-time at Honker Records. 7XI fell in love with the job and the whole concept of retail sales. Nobody knows how or why, including 7XI, but it happened. May have had something to do with her name. In no time 7XI was practically running the place while Bill cut back to 80 hours per week and returned to his martial arts regimen.

FOURTEEN

GROUND DOWN AROUND TOWN

WILSON AND I FANNED OUT ACROSS AMERICA to help out with our current projects, make sure upcoming job sites were equipped and prepared, fill our calendar with work for the upcoming year or so, and check in with our past clients. We gained all kinds of valuable information from our past clients and almost always received referrals to friends of people we'd worked with in the past. And those people are the best possible clients to work with. Wilson set Minnesota up for repeat success while I set off on a road trip from Los Angeles to Austin in a rented Kia. Arizona, New Mexico, Oklahoma, and then I decided I didn't want anything at all to do with Texas, I'd had enough of Hillbillyland, so I flew home to civilization.

"You look happy," Wilson said as we drove from the airport to Barney's Beanery.

"I'm not in Texas," I said.

"What was the highlight of the trip?" Wilson asked.

"Pauls Valley, Oklahoma. The Toy and Action Figure Museum."

"What was so great about that?"

"The Pez dispenser display."

"I've been to the Pez Museum. Somewhere in Silicon Valley, I think," Wilson said. "It was in a computer store."

"Sounds about right. I don't wanna live in America anymore," I told Wilson. "People everywhere seem compelled to wear their brainwashing as some kind of shield that prevents knowledge and information from penetrating their shattered souls."

"Where are you gonna go, then, if people everywhere are like that?" Wilson asked.

"There's a 7-11 in every country. It doesn't matter where you go as long as you go. As long as it isn't Texas. Fuck Texas."

FIFTEEN

THE BRAVE HEROES OF UVALDE, TEXAS

UVALDE, TEXAS, USA

377 TEXAS COPS STOOD OUTSIDE AN ELEMENTARY SCHOOL CLASSROOM FOR 77 MINUTES while a sick fuck murdered babies. People ask Black Patrick, "Why do you hate cops so much?" Please, read on. You might learn something today.

Part of the reason people who aren't stupid hate Texas is the cops in Texas. Cops are useless. I don't know if we ever remind those fortunate enough to serve us as police people what our expectations of them are. Cops have been programmed by generations of police union assholes to believe the most important part of their job is to get home safely to their families. That's not what we pay them for. We pay cops to serve us as courageous defenders of our freedom. Brave protectors of the people who pay them. Their job is to help us. When job number one is *officer safety*, we end up with Uvalde, Texas.

More useless pigs than can fit bagged, compacted, frozen, and stacked like firewood in a refrigerated shipping container destined for disposal on the bottom of the seafloor in the middle of the Pacific Ocean so as not to contaminate the soil anywhere near inhabited areas with the pathogenic coward genes endemic to cops stood outside Robb Elementary School while a lame cunt murdered 19 children and two adults. That's 377 cops lacking humanity, courage, and every single other attribute we need to see in a police officer. How those evil people were able to stand outside a classroom door for 77 minutes as gunshots blasted babies into oblivion is all we need to illustrate why we don't need American cops, in their current incarnation, any fucking more.

A sick and stupid group of 377 losers failed to take courageous action to stop the killing in Uvalde, Texas that day. Those 377 pieces of shit are emblematic of the other 708,000 pigs in the United States. American cops are cowards who prey on the weak, take those fat paychecks, benefits, and pensions home, and say, "Just doing my job." Just like the Nazis operating the gas chambers did. Fuck.

One kid in that Uvalde, Texas classroom survived while a classmate next to him died a long, slow death. Lasting memories of his friend's teeth all over the floor will haunt that dude for a lifetime. At one point, well into the cowardly, 77-minute-long cowering by the cops, a brave hero in a cute little outfit festooned with shiny things and patches designed to make little boys tingle, opened the door to the classroom and asked if there was anybody in there. A little girl answered, the coward closed the door, and four gunshots rang out inside the classroom as the child was executed. The poor little kid would likely be alive today were not for the absolute moron, loser, cop asking for volunteers to be murdered.

American cops are not only useless, they are extremely harmful to our society. Murderers. Thieves. Criminals. Thugs. And still, some people unwaveringly support their beloved and useless uniformed gang members. All the while pigs make a killing stealing our money and our freedom. The entire rotten system is filled with demented people propped up by even more demented people. Suckers.

Here's another way to look at Uvalde, Texas:

If there were no cops at Robb Elementary on May 24, 2022, do you think real people would have waited 77 minutes to go into that classroom and save those babies? Fuck. No. The fucking crossing guard would have risked her life to save a kid. Every single American cop is a coward trained to lie, cheat, and steal. Part of a uniformed, state-sanctioned, criminal enterprise operating with impunity. Figure it out. Don't be a dumbfuck your whole life.

L ET'S TALK ABOUT SOLUTIONS. A better way does exist. How do police officers operate in civilized countries? Well, as far as I can tell, policing in civilized societies focuses on helping people. Imagine that!

In Japan, for example, the culture of policing is non-violent.

Cops are largely seen in much the same way American people see their mail carriers—ubiquitous, friendly, helpful, kind, non-threatening, regular people. The opposite of the way every single American views every American cop.

American cops do everything they can to separate themselves from the non-cop population. A perfect example of that is the "blue line." At some point, pigs decided a blue line (blue symbolizing the color of many cop costumes) was an appropriate representation of their separation from others. Sure, the loser fucks will tell you it's the line where cops stand to protect the people from chaos. Sorry, you fucking liars, that's not it.

The blue line flag is a desecration of the American flag. Cop people feel entitled to desecrate our flag to demonstrate their separation from us. Get rid of that shit.

American cops wear silly vests with lots of pockets and Velcro-attached accessories containing vast amounts of items available at your local Staples and Walmart including, but not limited to:

Guns	Pens
Tasers	Paper
Gun magazines	Business cards
Scissors	Badges
Walkie-talkies	Name tags
Phones	Pepper spray
Handcuffs	Zip ties
Body-worn cameras	Billy clubs
Key rings	Flashlights
Sunglasses	

When was the last time you saw a cop use a pair of scissors to defend our freedoms? Those vests just make cops look even more stupid. Fuck that shit. If the everything-but-the-kitchen-sink Velcro vest made sense everybody would wear Velcro clothing so as to have every item necessary to complete every real and imaginary task readily at all times. I would be wearing a bottle opener, a flask, several drugs and the necessary drug paraphernalia, a roll of paper towels, a bottle of hot sauce, one of those Olive Garden cheese graters, guitar strings, and a megaphone. And a hammer. Because you never know when you'll need a hammer.

Back to Japan. In Japan you would encounter small neighborhood police stations called kōbans, unless you were an American, in which case you probably wouldn't have a passport. Unlike American police stations, kōbans are not fortresses ringed by barbed wire and staffed with push broom-mustached, cowardly, country music fans. Japan has more than 6,000 kōbans where people can walk in and report a crime, ask for directions, get help finding a hotel room, borrow money to get home, retrieve or deposit a lost or found item, or get help with a marital spat, among other things.

In Japan, cops don't hide from the people they work for in cars or behind barbed wire in fortresses. They're well aware their role in society is to HELP people, not harm people.

We need to make every American cop go away so we can start over. Odds are we'll need to make all of the friends and family of cops go away, as well. Where will they go? It doesn't matter where they go as long as it's away. Fuck those people.

SIXTEEN

A MAN NAMED DAVE

PASADENA, CALIFORNIA, USA

B ILL LOOKED LIKE HE'D FOUND THE SECRET SAUCE.

"I'm on fire!" Bill said as Wilson and I ambled into Pasadena's pantheon of phonography, Honker Records.

"Nice jumpsuit, man!" Wilson said.

"It's a flight suit, motherfucker. Flameproof, foolproof, dancin' on the sunroof, Doctor Rock!"

Somehow Bill's jive abilities had advanced substantially in our absence. That's not unusual. "The store looks fantastic, Bill. Where did you find all the supermodels?" I asked.

"Dave's house. Half the hot fashion students from the ArtCenter are over at his place every night."

"Who's Dave?"

"I didn't tell you?"

"Tell us what?"

As Bill tells it,   Bill was up at Devil's Gate Dam one day sporting his casual jumpsuit, relaxing in a beach chair reading Jacques Derrida's *Of Grammatology* when a random dude rolled up on his beach cruiser and said, "You can't do that here, man."

Bill peered over his tortoiseshell frames for a moment then returned to his studies, ignoring the bicycle-riding weirdo.

"You won't get any pussy criticizing Saussure around here."

Bill looked at the strange man dressed like a fighter pilot for a second and returned to his book. Bicycle man said, "I don't care if you're Jacque Cousteau, Jean-Jacque Rousseau, Haystack Balloon, Eric Bloom, you can't do that shit here, man."

Bill, again, peered over the top of his sunglasses and asked the bicycle man, "Do you know Bill Ham?"

"Bill Ham?" The man on the bicycle dismounted his two-wheeled machine, rubbed his hands together furiously, and then sang Bill a little song:

> *If you see me walkin' down the line*
> *With my favorite honky tonk in mind*
> *Well, I'll be here around suppertime*
> *With my can of dinner and a bunch of wine*
> *Beer drinkers and hell raisers, yeah*
> *Baby, don't you want to come with me?*

Bicycle Man picked up his transportation device, said, "No, never heard of the guy. See ya later, man," and rolled away on two wheels.

Unimpressed, Bill said, "You don't know Bill Ham," as Bicycle Man disappeared into the twilight.

Bill's fierce dedication to his staff and customers at Honker Records meant he never missed a day of work no matter how brutal the hangover—he knew how to play hurt, as the sports people say. The official Honker Records motto was, in fact, *Play Hurt*. Half-asleep behind the cash register counter Bill was disturbed by a familiar, enthusiastic voice.

Flight Suit Guy.

"We can't, we won't, we don't stop, Robbo! If it takes her an hour, a day, a week, or the whole wing of the fam damily to git 'er done!"

As Bill's hungover head rose from the ashes and above countertop level the store's most animated customer said, "God bless America! My man, you're alive and kickin'! Let's go!"

Jumpsuit Bill followed Flight Suit Guy on a bicycle journey to parts unknown—a rare, rare bookstore on a Pasadena side street. "Check this out, fifty grand," Flight Suit Guy said as he pulled an author-signed copy of a Winnie-the-Pooh book off the shelf.

"Burnt," Bill opined.

"Hey, man, I gotta run, jump to the dojo," Flight Suit Guy said. "See ya tomorrow." Since the rare bookstore was Barney's-adjacent happy hour started early.

Bill's favorite bartender, Stephanie, was behind the bar washing glassware in ways Bill's brain filed away for later use. "I'm thinking about buying my crew flight suits," Bill told Stephanie.

"Boo. Yoga pants," Stephanie suggested. "If I wore a flight suit to work I would never get any pussy."

"We sell records to Star Trek fans."

"That's because I don't work there," Stephanie said.

"Stephanie, you're hired. 2 hours a month, no flight suit. Tell me when you can work."

"Deal. You're a very intelligent and handsome man, Bill. Stop staring at my tits."

Bill got hammered and started internet shopping for hookers and military surplus clothing on his phone. He ordered Vietnamese to go and a dozen vintage flight suits for his crew, and one for his new homie. He also purchased a yoga romper for Stephanie, a decision that has come to be known as the greatest ever $20 investment in human history. Upon arrival,

Bill had a local artist screen print Honker's face on the back and above the front left-hand chest pocket on the flight suits. And an unobtrusive Honker on Stephanie's see-through yoga romper in the tramp stamp location.

Flight Suit Guy arrived at Honker HQ in a burst of rhyme and reason the next day as promised and advertised. He bought every Stevie Wonder album in stock, pointed across the sales floor at Billthy Animal, and proclaimed, "You're hungry, Kemosabe, time to get up for the chow down!"

Over empañadas at the Venezuelan restaurant, Bill learned Flight Suit Guy's name was Dave and he was between jobs studying to be a martial arts instructor. "How'd you get your hands on Cranberry?" Dave asked. "I tried to buy that place 40 years ago, 30 years ago, every year ago."

"Good timing, I guess. We're building a recording studio in the basement."

"What? That's amazing, man. I'll be your first client. I wanna do a sax album. Like Miles Davis. Let's go, it's time to blast some Stevie fuckin' Wonder."

"Great, thanks, Dave."

"Hold on. Kemosabe, before we go any further, we need to give you some mojo," flight suit guy Dave said.

"What kind of mojo?"

Dave pulled a magical device out of his fanny pack and sidled up to Bill on the bench seat. "Look in the mirror, Chief. What do you see?"

Bill said, with all confidence, "I see a champion in action."

Dave looked at Bill, nodded his approval, and said, "I see a guy who needs two things." Bill waited to hear the part about Dave's dick and Bill's mouth. "I see a guy who needs a haircut and an attitude. We're going to see Sensei Richard."

Bill was relieved when Dave's friend Richard turned out not to be his penis, but a hairstylist named Handsome Dick Manitoba.

Bill, with 50% more mojo, courtesy of Handsome Dick Manitoba.

Dave's house was a walled compound with a mansion, a huge lawn area, a pool and pool house, and a guest house. What was once a tennis court was now a beach filled with a foot of sand. The dynamic duo settled into the basement music room and listened to *Innervisions* at maximum volume. Dave asked Bill where he was living, Bill told him he was in an Airbnb, Dave said, "Not anymore, Doc, I need a brother to stay in the guest house for a while. There's business in Osaka I need to handle."

"Okay, I'll go get my shit. What do you want for rent?"

"Twenty-five cents a day," Dave answered.

Bill gave Dave $20, Dave gave Bill alarm codes and keys, and Dave was gone by the time Bill came back with his suitcase, Les Paul Junior, and an impressive collection of men's toiletries. Just another day in the life of Billthy Animal.

A couple of days later at work in the record store, Bill told Robbo he'd moved into record store regular Dave's guest house.

"No way!" Robbo said.

"Yeah, it's awesome. Dave turned a tennis court into a beach."

"You live in David Lee Roth's guest house? Fuck!"

"I do? I didn't know that was David Lee Roth. Dave has a pet owl."

SEVENTEEN

WHO BUILT THIS PLACE?

MICRONESIA

"YOU KNOW WHAT MICRONESIA NEEDS?" I asked Wilson. "Decent pizza?"

"Yeah, so does Los Angeles. Micronesia needs electric guitars. We need to hire the rest of Tropical Fuck Storm."

"That's wrong," Wilson J. Wilson said, "those guys need to be playing music, not wasting their time installing IKEA cabinets in underground panic rooms."

"Wilson, you're lucky you ever met me. Your limited imagination would have seen you building fire pits and turning front yards into driveways for dumbfucks in El Sereno and Cypress Park your whole life. Look where you are now."

"Fuck you."

"We're hiring Tropical Fuck Storm to perform live on a barge in the lagoon outside Taz's bar. Loud as fuck, fireworks, dancing women, the whole deal. Jumbotron, free booze, Goodyear blimp..."

"You know what'll happen after that?" Wilson asked.

"We go to prison?"

"No, the chief will demand we bring rock 'n' roll to Nan Madol."

"Rock 'n' Roll Nan Madol. That's a tremendous idea. Wilson, this LSD is amazing."

A film crew accompanied Tropical Fuck Storm on its voyage from Nagambie to Micronesia. Upon arrival in Pohnpei, celebrations commenced on Taz Mountain. Rehearsals in the bunker with long-lost drummer Hammer imbued the blank concrete cube with warmth and soul. The walls, floors, and bombproof lid of the bunker roared to life as a living, breathing, partying organism. We blasted Stevie Wonder, Motörhead, Howlin' Wolf, Parliament, and Discharge down there at full volume as we smoked weed. After we listened to side one of *Van Halen* at Wilson's insistence, our work seasoning the bunker was done. We declared victory, parted company with our bunker brother, and named him Steve.

Tropical Fuck Storm spent the week leading up to their show rehearsing, traveling the island, meeting people, learning, and loving every minute of it. We all visited the chief in Nan Madol and requested his presence at Tropical Fuck Storm's show. The chief told the members of Tropical Fuck Storm his favorite band was AC/DC. The band told Taz they needed cannons on the mountains above the lagoon for their encore, a cover of "For Those About to Rock." Taz set it up.

By the time Tropical Fuck Storm stepped on their floating concert stage. every person on the island, and more than a few on neighboring islands, recognized they were in the presence of Nagambie's greatest band. Word spread, the "Braindrops" video from Nagambie Speedway streamed on YouTube made brains drop, and the local vernacular henceforth included terms such as, "You let my tyres down."

The greatest band on the planet.

Tropical Fuck Storm murdered half of Pohnpei's population with their insanely great performance. The band absorbed the essence of the Pohnpeians and reflected it upon their hosts in a most magnificent way. Honorary titles and offers of virgins and giant fish followed in the wake of

Tropical Fuck Storm's legendary concert. Lax security at the airport saw throngs of Tropical Fuck Storm fans sprinting down the runway chasing the band as the United Airlines 737 lifted off from Pohnpei heading back to a place where they were no longer prince and princesses.

"That was the greatest thing I've ever seen in my entire life," Taz said. "People of all ages going absolutely mental appreciating every moment of Tropical Fuck Storm."

"Do you think they delivered a good set?" I asked Taz.

Taz knew I was joking, but he still wanted to kill me. "Pohnpei will never be the same. Every dude wants a red Fender Jaguar, girls want drums, guitars, bass guitars, and synthesizers."

"Taz, we're opening a musical instrument store here. Everything's a dollar."

"How can we afford to do that?"

"The movie will make millions. Remember the guy in charge of the film crew?"

"Yeah."

"That was Martin."

"Steve?"

"Scorsese. Steve is your bunker."

What happened on Pohnpei was incredible. There was no money to be made by an invading rock band. There were no minerals to steal from the natives. Tropical Fuck Storm took from Pohnpei a deep and lifelong understanding of real people. People in Pohnpei learned to use the electric guitar to communicate their awesomeness to each other. If any of that translated to worldwide success in rock 'n' roll we haven't heard about it. And fuck anyone who believes that's the measure of a band or a person's value. "Yay, a bunch of people I'll never know think I'm cool!"

"That's meaningless, Tim," I said to America's most famous child-molesting faux punk rocker when I saw him shopping at Honker Records.

"Are you talking to me, motherfucker?" Tim asked.

"Tim, don't you have a 14-year-old in your basement who misses her daddy?"

"Maybe."

"Your band sucks. Your music is terrible and I am politely asking you to go the fuck away. Forever."

"But I like touring the world and fucking pre-teen girls."

"I'll just tell you this, Timmy. You've been fucking the wrong 12-year-olds. If you'd been fucking the right 12-year-olds your music would reflect that."

"I did everything right. I hired Ted Nugent's road manager—"

"Tell me about your relationship with Gary Glitter."

"Gary was into some weird shit with people who said, 'After eight it's too late,' before every shot at the bar. I told Gary, 'After nine, it's my time,' and after that, we got along just fine."

"So, age nine was a gap year?"

In conclusion, Tim's band is the worst band the world has ever seen. Posers. Every fan of Tim's band is a cunt who has never listened to a Bootsy Collins solo record. I know, hard to believe people are walking the face of Earth who don't know what we all need to know to function in conjunction with Star Child.

EIGHTEEN

HONKER ON SAFARI

AFRICA

DAVE SHOT BACK INTO TOWN AND SURPRISED HIS TENANT, Bill, in the guest house while Bill attempted to light the pilot light of the floor furnace.

"Get up for the downstroke, Billthy. You, my friend, are nominated and vaccinated. Prepare to be resuscitated, we're leaving for Africa right now."

And, with that, Bill and Dave were off to the airport. "Where are we going, exactly?" Bill asked.

"Mahonda Mkataleni, hombre. Strap in and hold on tight."

"Where's that?"

"Unguja."

"Where's that?"

"Zanzibar."

"Where's that?"

"Tanzania."

"Where's that?"

"Africa."

"Okay."

"We hit the ground in Zanzibar and head straight to my school, Chief," Dave told Bill.

"You have a school in Africa?"

"Several, we only have time for one on this trip, it pains me to say. Then we hit Dar es Salaam because my business manager needs me to say hihowareya to our African benefactors, then, it's off to hang with the baboons."

"I hear baboons spend most of their time just hangin' around."

"Have you been tested?" Dave asked.

"No more bareback, Dave. How was Osaka?"

"Incredible, Bill. Those cosplay babes are insatiable and unbelievable."

"I believe you're unable to satisfy Japanese women, based on your account of events."

"Fuck you, Billy Bob. I spent a week in the dojo teaching senseis mojo."

"Can you teach mojo?"

"Yes, however, they will never learn. There is no Japanese Howlin' Wolf. I pontificate, elaborate, and demonstrate, but it doesn't resonate. There's a reason the Rolling Stones weren't born in Japan."

"Black Patrick and Wilson just got back from Micronesia. They brought a band from Australia to Pohnpei and introduced the island people to live rock 'n' roll."

"I saw some video. I must say, very impressive. The cannons on the hillside, epic. The band—incredible. The world needs more dissonance."

"Wilson said something about building a recording studio for the chief near Nan Madol."

"Absolutely not, Billy. That's some bad juju out there. Those spirits are on a hairline trigger—it's palpable the moment of arrival. That's sacred ground out there. The entrance to an even more magical place we can't even imagine."

Bill + Mushrooms.
"There's a bright golden haze on the meadow…"

Bill is nothing if not a thoughtful and generous man. On the first of a few flights required to reach Mahonda Mkataleni, Bill had a surprise for Dave. "I brought you a present, Dave,"

Bill said as he retrieved his carry-on bag from the overhead storage bin and pulled out a Honker Records gift bag.

"Aw, man, that's somethin' else. Early '80s, West Germany," Dave said as he examined the vintage flight suit festooned with Honker livery. "Yes! Thank you, Bill. Thank you,"

"We just got the Honker patches in. I brought my flight suit, too," Bill said.

Dave was visibly impressed and moved by Bill's kind gesture "It's truly special, man. Beautiful in every way. Thanks, man. We're wearing these on safari."

Bill described Dave's school in Zanzibar, The Roth Academy of Extraordinary Individuals, in a way that struck me as a place I would have looked forward to being every day as a kid. Kids started the day with breakfast while watching an episode of SpongeBob SquarePants. Then the first segment of classroom action featured a brief presentation by a local business owner or politician or musician or farmer talking about real-world shit. Then the students broke out into two academic sessions before lunch. As lunch was served students listened to music selected by the school's namesake. Another academic session followed lunch, then an hour for an elective class. Then a brief technology session.

After the structured part of the day, the students did whatever they wanted to do—music, art, sports, and horticulture are examples of some of what Bill saw going on. Students were required to set goals and demonstrate achievement of those objectives. The whole place was reportedly alive and buzzing with positive energy and great juju. That's what happens when people start their day with SpongeBob.

In Dar es Salaam Dave met with the philanthropists funding his schools in Tanzania while Bill held court at the hotel pool. Dave returned from his meeting and told Bill, "Change of plans, big guy, we are going to see the cave elephants in Kenya."

"Cave elephants? When did elephants start living in caves?" Bill asked.

"When the elephants figured out their hidden talents as miners. Thousands of years ago," said Professor Roth. "The cave elephants are forest elephants who visit the caves at night to scrape the walls with their tusks so they can eat chunks of rock that fall off. The elephants need the salt and other minerals in the cave's walls because the rains wash away all the minerals in the soil."

Bill thought about the whole, wacky, concept and quipped, "I wonder how they figured that out."

Dave insisted he and Bill wear their Honker flight suits at all times in Kenya. In the Nairobi airport, the locals gave the pair strange looks and seemed to scoff. Children pointed and screamed at Bill, in particular. "That's normal around here, hombre," Dave said, "just like Alabama, where the tusks are looser" On the drive from Kitale to Mount Elgon, home of cave elephants, Dave, Bill and the Kenyan posse from Uganda stopped in a village with food Dave's remembrance from past visits regarded as, "Better than any taco truck in Kentucky!"

Dave's old friends at the roadside cafe toasted his arrival with waragi and the national beer of Kenya, Tusker Lager.

"What's waragi?" Bill asked Dave.

"Chang'aa. Drink a lot of it or you're being rude to our hosts."

And that's what Bill did. When food arrived Bill dove in and told Dave, "This shit is incredible, man."

Dave asked, "Do you like the dik-dik?"

"What's that?"

"It's the meat. It's dik-dik. A dik-dik is a tiny antelope the size of a cat."

"Yes," Bill answered, "more dik-dik!"

Bill excused himself to use the restroom facilities and got lost in the jungle. After he relieved himself on a banana tree and before he could finish figuring out how to fasten his flight suit a giant, ugly, smelly beast resembling the Motörhead mascot announced its presence and signaled anger. Bill screamed and ran through the jungle and, by the grace of Lemmy, straight through the restaurant patio and into the posse's safari ride. The crew looked at him like he was a madman until a dozen giant forest hogs charged the group, sending screaming people scurrying in every direction.

"They never do that," our driver said once everybody was back in the car. "They never do that."

Bill couldn't help but admit, "It must have been the dik-dik."

At the gates to Mount Elgon National Park Dave was greeted like a global explorer returning as a hero, Bill reported. People danced, played joyous music, and presented Dave with flowers and gifts. Women threw themselves at him. I saw the video.

Dave informed Bill of the schedule of safari events. "The elephants arrive tomorrow, Bill. Hold on to your toupee."

"Are the elephants on a schedule?" Bill asked.

"Maybe, but we know when they'll hit the caves by the temperature of the dung." Dave explained, "The rangers found a lukewarm deposit about 7 clicks out, and a steaming pile 3 clicks away from the caves."

"Cool," Bill said. "I'll take a nap, then."

"No can do. We're drivin' and cryin' to zebra town. Let's go!"

"Never fuck with a zebra," Dave said as a herd of Zebras appeared through the windshield. "A zebra will bite your arm off. If he doesn't kick the shit out of you first."

Bill told Dave, "I have never heard a good thing about a zebra." Just as Bill, Dave, and their safari guides exited the vehicle and admired a group of six zebras the crazy black-and-white-striped horses made evil-sounding noises and ran straight at them. The lead zebra stopped in front of the vehicle and stared intently at the frightened humans inside for a good fifteen seconds.

The driver said, again, "They never do that." Followed a little while later by, "I quit," as we exited his vehicle back at our cottage. He drove away and may or may not have ever been seen again.

That evening a contingent from the local community arrived bearing food and beverage, Bill and Dave were treated like a king and queen. The next day the dynamic duo went for a hike and were told by a ranger their new driver would arrive in the evening. When their driver/guide hadn't arrived by the late afternoon they hiked to a spot where the elephants could be observed on their way to the caves. As the herd passed by them about 50 yards away, one particularly observant elephant with bullet holes in its ears stopped and stared at Dave and Bill for a long time. Dave and Bill ran as fast as they could. They were followed by the sound of a thundering herd of elephants behind them.

Back at their home away from home, a guy in a beat-up Land Cruiser was checking the fluids under the hood. Dave yelled something in Swahili, the man slammed the hood, jumped in the vehicle, and started the engine. Bill and Dave grabbed their belongings and joined their new best friend on a three-hour trip to the nearest city with an Irish pub.

At Tanzania's only Irish pub inside a hotel inside a shopping mall, the bartender asked, "Where did you get such demonic clothing?"

Dave wasted no time answering, "From the demons! This is vintage gear! Bought and sold over and over again by demons."

The bartender said, "There was a demon here fifteen years ago who looked just like that devil on your pajamas. He raped, tortured, and massacred many people in the caves."

"Where?" Bill asked.

"Mt. Elgon. Do not go near any elephants wearing that stupid romper. Elephants never forget."

Dave finally told Bill, "There was a war here a while back, es no mas, amigo."

"That elephant who charged at us had bullet holes in his ears," Bill said.

"The insurgents kidnapped people, hung them from trees, tortured them, and stole all their shit," Dave said. "But it gets worse."

Bill asked, "Wait, there's still more?"

"The guy who looked like Honker would cut your ear off and make you eat it."

Never one to miss an opportunity, Bill said, "Vincent van Honker."

<&>

Five or six different flights later, Dave and Bill arrived at Pasadena's famous Casa de Dave exhausted. "Where did the guest house go?" Bill asked Dave.

"Good question," Dave replied as he viewed the charred parcel in Pasadena where a structure once stood. Dave called his neighbor, Neil deGrasse Tyson.

Neil answered the phone, "Welcome back, Dave! Your guest house blew up!" followed by ten seconds of that husky guffaw Neil has.

"How?"

"Loudly. Scientifically speaking, the building went ka-boom. And then it went away."

"Where did it go?" Dave asked.

"I called 1-800-GOT-JUNK for you and they delivered your steaming pile of wreckage to the dump. You owe me $2,600. The fire department said it happens all the time. Probably a gas leak."

Bill knew exactly why the guest house went ka-boom, but he was never going to tell anyone. The guy who left the heater on full blast without the pilot light lit put the most positive spin possible on the situation. "Wow! That's a great price to haul away a whole guest house!"

<&>

WHILE BILL AND DAVE HAD BEEN OFF ON SAFARI, Bill's superstar manager from Mistake Records in San

Clemente, Ivy, took over Honker Records and put her stamp on it. Whilst retaining everything that made Honker Records so awesome and successful, Ivy and new sidekick, 7XI, managed to create a vibe that brought all the ladies around, just as she had done in San Clemente. Sales volume increased dramatically within a few short weeks; none of us could figure out how she was doing it; Bill stayed out of the way and let her fill the bank account with cash and the store with Taylor Swift fans.

Ivy and 7XI proposed a brilliant store-within-a-store concept called IV7XI in a chunk of the retail space. Whatever they asked for, the answer was always yes, it always worked.

Right around this time the owner of the building next door to us told Bill he wanted to sell it. In the blink of an eye we locked the property down with an option to purchase it. Good times.

PART 3
MEAN MACHINE

BLACKWATER INVASION

A S SOON AS BILL AND DAVE RETURNED FROM AFRICA it was time to put my ambitious plan for Honker Studios in action.

"Colton, let me put somebody on the phone with you," I told my Blackwater Sales Engineer.

"Colton. My name is Dave. I live in Pasadena, California. I am a single, successful man of many more mysteries than stars in the clear Minnesota sky. My man, Patrick, informs me I need to meet your chief."

"Okay. I'll make it happen."

Dave handed me back the phone, grabbed his bootstraps, and headed out the door on a beach cruiser built to travel intergalactically.

"Thanks, man," Dave said. "Set the date and we'll see you then."

"Who was that guy?" Colton asked.

"David Lee Roth."

"Holy fuck! Chip will shit when he meets David Lee Roth."

"Don't tell anyone. Just get us the meeting. I'm sending you a selfie so you know, without a doubt, we are serious," because nothing says *serious* like a selfie with David Lee fucking Roth.

"Thank you, Patrick. Why do you want to meet with Chip?" Colton asked.

"For the same reason I've been telling you for years now. A female-friendly recording studio. We have a 7,000-square-foot basement space we're turning into a state-of-the-art, female-friendly recording studio complex. We want to partner with Blackwater and do something new."

"Oh, that one. What makes a recording studio female-friendly?" Colton asked.

"How the fuck would I know? Clean bathrooms? A lack of sketchy dudes working there? Fresh flowers? A mechanical bull? Who knows? We have females around here to make those decisions."

"That's a good thing. I'll call you right back."

My female-friendly recording studio concept was absolutely serious. Serious as a heart attack. The majority of new guitar players are ladies. That means most people buying a guitar for the first time are female. The typical guitar store is a shitty experience for all people of all genders. The recording studio experience is likely a whole lot worse from the feminine perspective. Hence my billion-dollar idea and our current endeavor.

Blackwater was and remains the largest online retailer of musical equipment in the world. Other than their retail store and studio complex in Duluth, Minnesota their physical customer interface was entirely online or via telephone. My sales pitch to Chip would be an opportunity for Blackwater to expose themselves to girls. Wait, that didn't exactly come out the way it was intended.

Blackwater sales engineers don't fuck around, our meeting was on. I called Wilson, "Oh, boy. Hey, W, we need to leave for the airport in six hours."

"Okay."

Then I called Bill, "Bill, we're leaving for the airport in 6 hours. Bring Ivy and 7XI. Call Dave and see if he can make it."

"Okay."

Remarkably five of us synchronized our lives in a way that resulted in success. Dave was on his way to Papua New Guinea so he wouldn't be joining us in person.

We landed in Minneapolis, drove straight to the Blackwater campus, and had breakfast at the Blackwater cafeteria. When the massive gear store opened we went our separate ways in the gigantic Blackwater Megastore for an hour or so until we all needed a drink. On the way out Wilson bought a Taylor acoustic, 7XI picked up a Rickenbacker bass, Ivy bought a gold top Les Paul, Bill bought a Korg synth for himself and a vocal foot pedal for

Dave, and I bought a Walrus delay pedal I'd never be able to figure out. And I secretly purchased a used Joan Jett Gibson Melody Maker as a birthday present for 7XI.

At the finest bar and grill near Blackwater headquarters, our gang was shitfaced almost instantly. Bill asked, "Why are we here, again?" I guess we forgot to talk about that.

"We have a meeting at 4 p.m. with the CEO of Blackwater."

"Chip Conrad?" Ivy asked.

"Yep, the chief. We want him to give us all the gear for the studio."

"Will he do that?" 7XI asked.

"Yes."

"Why?" Bill asked.

"I'll handle that part. You guys need to be upbeat, high-energy, excited, and your usual awesome selves. Strong. Focused. After the hellos don't say shit unless Chip asks you a question. I've been working on this concept for 5 years, I can't believe we're here."

"More tequila!" Wilson insisted.

Time to tour the Blackwater Studio complex. "Dave couldn't make it," I told Blackwater Sales Engineer, Colton. "We'll FaceTime him at 4:30."

"Chip will lose his mind.," Colton said. "Dave is his hero. Chip quotes Dave in our companywide meetings almost every time."

"We need you and Chip to come see us in California. That's our only goal here—to set that appointment."

Colton said, "Don't include me or he'll make me go so he doesn't have to."

"Good point. That's why you're the best goddamn sales engineer on the planet."

I told Chip we wanted him to come see us in Pasadena. Chip said, "I'll be there in ten days. My friends at Rickenbacker need to see me, I don't know why, but when Rickenbacker wants to see me, I go. It's Rickenbacker. Rickenbacker! I don't give a shit about anything more than Rickenbacker. None of this shit would be here without Rickenbacker."

Chip, Champ, and Bill engaged in an intellectual conversation regarding the pros and cons of various pizza toppings.

"Wow…" Wilson said.

"What's wrong with 7XI?" Chip asked.

We all turned around to see 7XI hiding her face as tears eroded her makeup turning eyeliner into a river of ink stains on Chip's area rug. "7XI bought your only 4003 in stock," I told Chip. "She loves everything Rickenbacker. She's really nervous and you just broke her brain."

"7XI, you're coming with me to Rickenbacker," Chip said. "Colton, take these three knuckleheads to Knuckledragger's for drinks and wings then meet me at my place, we're having a barbecue. I need to talk to Wilson and Patrick."

Chip led Wilson and me out the secret side door from the office to his car, and within 10 minutes we were airborne in his Cessna. "Sorry I made your friend cry," Chip said.

"We've never seen her like that," Wilson said.

"I have," I said.

"7XI has great admiration for you and your company and you just took that to another level," Wilson said. "Thank you, Chip."

"Shit!" I exclaimed from the back seat of Chip's flying lawnmower. "We forgot to FaceTime Dave."

"Dave who?" Chip asked.

"Let's land first," Wilson said.

Chip said, "I want you to build me a doomsday bunker. I have a 15,000-square-foot dining hall with a 15,000-square-foot basement underneath. I want two levels under there as far below that as you can go."

"We will have a proposal for you by the end of the day tomorrow," Wilson said.

Chip landed his Cessna on what looked to me like a peat bog next to his complex of buildings in the middle of nowhere. "I have 428 acres here, nobody knows or cares what I do," Chip said as we crossed a bridge leading from one of his islands to another. "I should buy a jet."

We walked into a hunting lodge-type building and I FaceTimed Dave. Dave's voice exploded out of my phone, "Chief Black Patrick, to what or whom do I owe the honor, señor?"

"Dave, you're never going to believe who me and Wilson are with right now."

Chip didn't immediately realize who Dave was, and said, "Hello Dave, I'm Chip Conrad." After a moment of silence, Dave went ballistic with effusive praise and noted events and accomplishments from Chip's life only stalkers would know.

"David Lee Roth?" Chip said to no one in particular. "Who the fuck are you people?"

Chip and Dave conversed while Wilson and I finished a bottle of scotch and wondered what the hell was going on. Dave excused himself to hammer a tribal tattoo into the back of the chief of whatever tribe he belonged to in Papua New Guinea, then Chip fired up the barbecue in silence as Wilson and I scouted the property for the best spot to plant a doomsday bunker.

"You don't understand," Chip said as he stared at the steaks on the grill. "That was like the world's biggest Beatles fan talking to Paul McCartney. I'm stunned."

"Chip, you've only known us an hour," I said. "This kind of shit happens all day, every day on our planet."

Chip insisted Wilson and I hang out with him for a few days. We finalized plans to build him a bunker, met dozens of Chip's homies, gained insight into the machinations of the Blackwater juggernaut, and then parted ways as Wilson and I returned to California and Chip flew to Nashville. What a bummer to say goodbye to Chip. We knew, however, we'd be seeing him again in a few days on our home turf.

"Dave's back," I told Wilson. "When Chip's in Pasadena, we'll have five minutes with Chip until the Chip 'n' Dave bromance goes nuclear."

"Chip's in the posse," Wilson said. "We know it when we see it. Like Hammer. Life's a lot simpler when you can see the value in people before you even know their name or say a word."

"Have you been reading *Crazy from the Heat*?"

"Yeah, but that kind of spiritual mumbo jumbo isn't in Dave's book, I learned that in Narcotics Anonymous."

The rumble of a Rickenbacker through an Ampeg SVT rattled the windows of my Uber and put a big smile on my face as I arrived at my humble abode. The neighbors told me 7XI hadn't stopped slamming the 'hood with her new Rickenbacker since she returned from Minnesota. I was impressed to hear her deft deployment of flanger and wah as I opened the door to the detached garage and laid eyes on the hottest bass player not in Mercyful Fate. Call me Becky. I'm around.

Before 7XI could see me I closed the door and crashed on the couch in the detached house. The knowledge that everybody in the posse was happy, healthy, firing on all cylinders, and flying through the stratosphere on a rocket ship meant everything, man.

A few days later we picked up Chip from the airport and took him straight to the basement under Honker and IV7XI. In the darkness, the silhouette of a man swinging a sword around was barely visible. The sword guy stopped, walked up to Chip, handed him his sword, and said, "Feel this. The weight. The simplicity. The honesty. I want a microphone made out of this steel."

And that was that. Chip may or may not have seen the basement. He had a chance to meet Robbo and say hello to Bill, 7XI, and Ivy again, then Dave, Chip, and my 19-year-old girlfriend roared out of the parking lot on a mission to see the Rickenbackers.

"When did everything turn so dramatic?" Wilson asked.

I knew. "Remember that day a fire tornado wiped out the birthing center next door to your house?"

About ten days later Chip called me. "Patrick, can you keep a secret?"

"All day long, Chip."

"Dave took me, the Rickenbackers, and your girlfriend to Tijuana. Your girlfriend applied for a job at Hong Kong Bar and was still going through the interview process when we left."

"It happens."

"I got hammered and bought Rickenbacker, And then the Rickenbackers disappeared."

"Is Dave alright?"

"That crazy fucker is on one of those janky old buses with 50 trumpet players all wearing the same silly Mexican cowboy outfit touring Mexico right now. I hung in there as long as I could and got on a bus back to Tijuana."

"That's badass."

"I lost my wallet, my phone, and one of my shoes. Get me out of this place."

"Tell me where you are and I'll send an Uber. You'll go to the San Diego airport and fly to Burbank. What size shoes do you wear?"

"Ten"

"Congratulations! You own a Rickenbacker!"

"Is Rickenbacker Mexican for donkey?"

Sounded like Chip had been through the wringer. I picked Chip up at the airport and we pointed the car to Dave's house where Bill, Wilson, and Ivy were waiting to welcome Chip back to America. Chip jumped in the pool with all his clothes on then joined Bill on the tennis court Dave filled with sand to create a beach.

"Bill, is this real or isn't it real? Because if it's not real that's fine by me. I've got plenty of things to do."

"Oh, it's real, big time, Chip. Ivy's Swifties are on the way. Dave just texted. The tour bus is comin' in hot. See that guy over there digging a hole in the lawn?"

"It looks like a grave," Chip said.

"We're having a luau."

"7XI is a hooker in Tijuana now," Chip reported.

"God bless America."

"She can suck the chrome off a trailer hitch."

"7XI is a champion in action. Sometimes I'm not even sure she's human," Bill said.

"She's a little bit Dr. Doolittle, too," Chip revealed. "Bill, I got fucked up in Tijuana and bought Rickenbacker. I have no idea how it happened."

"Cool, Patrick told me. A bass or a guitar?"

"The whole company. All of it. I'm totally fucked. What the hell do I do with that place? It's like a retirement home for guitar builders."

"Send Black Patrick down there to run Rickenbacker," Bill advised. "He loves Orange County."

"Good idea. I'm announcing his appointment to the CEO position right now."

"Don't tell him."

"We have to tell him," Chip said.

"Let Dave tell him."

<◈>

The tour bus announced its presence outside the walls of Dave's compound with a horn blast resembling that of a taco truck followed by a hand-cranked air raid siren. Dave leapt out first wearing warpaint and a shimmering Mexican polka band outfit. He let out a sound not unlike a jet engine passing overhead and waved to the neighbors as he directed an unending stream of men in identical outfits down the steps of the bus, through the gates of the compound, and directly toward the man ripping meat from pig bones.

"Let me introduce you to this fine 1979 MCI MC-9 47-passenger international assault vehicle," Dave announced. "Everything you need except an extra toilet or three."

"I didn't know you had a Greyhound stop here," Wilson said.

Dave informed us, "There isn't enough room on the bus for everyone so we don't hire a driver. The tuba player almost killed us. Twice"

"That's a large instrument," Chip told Dave as he excused himself to take selfies with the brass section.

"The band's chowin' down and staying at hotels in Eagle Rock. Tomorrow night we start recording in my living room. Mobile on the way from Las Vegas splashin' down in a few. Four days before the band leaves for Oaxaca. November means a week of shows with yours truly in Mexico, then a week of shows all over Los Angeles. And another record."

"We're opening the studio December 1st no matter what. You can record it there."

"Perfect. We're doing a cover of 'Beer Drinkers and Hell Raisers' live."

"Bill will lose his mind. Tell Chip you need some microphones and shit."

"I need to give Chip some cash," Dave said.

"Why?"

"We used his credit card to pay for everything in Mexico. Everything. That's a new bus. And the Vegas mobile unit. Must be fifty grand, total, minimum."

Dave had a pow-wow with Chip, from all appearances important business was discussed and agreements were reached. Dave went inside his house, returned with a giant megaphone, and demanded attention.

"Ladies and gentlemen and Felix, as you are well aware, the magnificent Mr. Conrad and myself visited a place called Meh-hee-co! (cheers, whistles, party horns) We stumbled into a bar and met the greatest band of maniacs Mexico has ever seen! As the band boarded the bus, drum god, Jesus, told me, 'Get on the bus, David Lee Roth.' I grabbed Chip and we didn't look back!"

"Is that what happened?" I asked Chip.

"I don't remember," he answered.

"We played 15 shows in a week all over Mexico, I've never had more fun on a tour in my life! Morning shows, afternoon shows, middle-of-the-night bar mitzvahs, quinceañeras, halftime shows, parades—it was amazing! The show has started! One more thing. Chip wanted me to announce our new venture, Blackwater Dave Records, the signing of our band to Blackwater Dave Records, and Black Patrick's new job—CEO Blackwater / Rickenbacker!"

<＠>

"How the fuck did I just become the CEO of Rickenbacker?" I asked Wilson. "I hate Orange County."

"The same way your girlfriend became a hooker in Tijuana. You can't get enough," Wilson answered.

"My girlfriend's a hooker in Tijuana?"

"Yeah, her pimp drives Dave's car now."

"I don't give a fuck about anything but Rickenbacker right now."

"Rickenbacker is a failing company, you will never be able to afford to pay yourself what you make at EAD. Not even close."

"I don't give a fuck about Rickenbacker anymore."

<＠>

Although Chip was slurring his words and looked like he'd had a recent stroke, his ability to spot a moneymaker was unaffected. "Patrick, Wilson, I don't know what the fuck you guys have going on around here. But I'm not missing out on it. I sent your list of gear to Colton, it'll all be here late October / early November."

"Wow, that's amazing, Chip," Wilson said.

"We're sending technicians to install everything, every manufacturer will send reps here to make sure you have the gear and training you need, don't be shy about asking for more. Colton's your point man, he's here the second week of

November. I just spoke with some of the people in the industry who sent the search party to Tijuana, everyone is really excited and I am too. We don't know why, but something feels right."

"Thank you, Chip," I said.

Wilson asked Chip, "Do you need to go to the hospital?"

All of the studio plans discussed with Chip incorporated the building next door, so we immediately exercised our option, closed the sale as fast as we could, helped the printing company move out, and began its conversion to Honker Records. IV7XI's incredible success meant the original Honker Records spot would convert to a stand-alone IV7XI store.

TWENTY

TO KILL A MOTHERFUCKING MOCKINGBIRD

ORANGE COUNTY

THE NEW GIG AT RICKENBACKER felt more like a hospice facility manager than the CEO of a guitar company. "Wilson, why are people in their 80s such assholes?"

"Because they think they're special. The largest segment of useless people are those between the ages of 80 and 89. The octogenarians of today are beneficiaries of the Great Generational Theft Project."

"Why don't we call Philthy and borrow his hammer? There's one motherfucker, in particular, I need to kill, and Philthy's hammer will make him die."

"Philthy's hammer is a good start. Have you tried the Hamas Sharp Shovel Decapitation Method?" Wilson asked.

"No. That's more of an already-dead decapitation method, right?"

"That's the mistaken impression many people have. Given that your blade is sharp enough, and you're using a square spade, the neck wound looks like it's buffed and polished. It's beautiful. Like glass. As you know, spade decapitations are typically performed with the old fuck prone on his back. The Hamas Sharp Spade Decapitation Method is frequently and effectively employed on standing targets facing in any direction."

"I wanna try that one," I said.

"Have you tried the new baseball bat decapitation sword? If you swing the bat faster than 300 miles per hour and hit the neck just right, the head stays on the torso for a moment after it's been severed."

"I think that's called the Neil deGrasse Tyson."

"Touché."

<⊛>

"Wilson, I don't know how to tell you this. I'm thinking about killing myself today. Everybody I know seems to be engaged in a competition to be the biggest asshole."

"What does that trophy look like?"

"Good question. The Biggest Asshole Cup is a 1/8th scale American Standard Reliant Two-Piece 10 inch."

"That's a nice piece of porcelain. I'm a big fan of the American Standard Slow-Close Seat."

"I've tried all of the 17-inch tall American Standards with elongated bowls—you can't go wrong there."

"1.6 gallons is the only way to go."

TWENTY-ONE

GROW UP AND GET A JOB!

A PHONE CALL WITH A SICK MAN

MY LIFE PLANS NEVER QUITE INCLUDED THIS. Somebody once told me, "God laughs hardest when one makes plans." Whatever.

Not long before my fortunate meeting with Wilson, multiple, compounding medical conditions rendered me somewhat incapacitated, incapable of walking and performing many activities required to perform tasks related to most types of employment. The kindness of my wealthy employer and the sale of my most valuable asset—a 2012 Toyota Prius C—assisted me through much of that dark period. Without the company's aid, food, shelter, and transportation to doctors' appointments would not have been available to me. For all of their help, I remain eternally grateful.

A few days after the calendar invented by a child molesting pope announced the need to add a different four-digit number to mark a period of time, my landlord sent me a text:

> Your company says they can't continue to support you they told me.
> What is the plan Patrick?
> Please communicate by tomorrow

Okay, no problem. I'll figure something out, I thought to myself. *And, if I don't, no problem, I live in a tall building.* Asking anyone for help was always difficult for me to do. By that point, I was worn out, over it all, and living in acceptance. I felt I owed it to my friends and those who cared about me to explain why I would likely be unavailable henceforth. And the writer in me felt compelled to document this episode in my life.

I hadn't reached out to the bastard since my descent into suicidal depression began. "HI, I'm not calling to ask you to reconsider your decision, I just want to know why you've decided to stop helping me through this difficult time."

"IT'S TIME FOR YOU TO GROW UP AND GET A *JOB!*" the angry little man on the other end of the line screamed in his best Sam Kinison voice.

"Are you fucking kidding me, motherfucker? Fuck you! I can't walk, I'm dealing with heart failure, arthritis in my hip and knee, and I have this neurological deal that makes me tremble all the time."

"IT'S YOUR *FAULT!*"

"Fuck you, you fucking asshole! Do you really think heart failure, arthritis, and this genetic tremor condition are my fault? You're a fucking cunt."

"GO TO THE *DOCTOR!*"

"I've been, I'm going again in March."

"I CAN'T AFFORD TO PAY FOR YOU ANYMORE! YOU NEED TO GET A *JOB!*"

"I'm sorry to hear that. Are you bankrupt?"

"I'M HAVING TO USE MY SAVINGS TO PAY FOR YOU!"

And, because he's an asshole, this broke guy said, "Well, maybe you should have managed your money better."

The bitter old bastard did answer my question, dishonestly, I presume, so I can communicate the essence of his Ill Communication when the time comes. He also said, "I'M PAYING YOUR RENT THIS MONTH BUT THAT'S IT." I didn't ask him to do that. I don't care anymore. I would rather die than ever speak with that spiritually dead man again. What a dick.

TWENTY-TWO

MISTER LEE! SIT DOWN! EAT!

SEOUL, SOUTH KOREA

"WILSON, DO YOU WANT TO KNOW WHY I STOPPED DATING ASIAN WOMEN?" I asked my traveling partner.

"DD is 25% Asian."

"She is? Why didn't you tell me?"

"You don't need to know most of the things I know that you don't know."

"Anyway, I was married to a woman—"

"A woman?"

"Fuck you. I was married to a woman," I continued, "and we traveled to a place called Seoul, South Korea so she could introduce me to her extended family. We brought a bottle of whiskey as a gift. While nobody was looking, my wife's grandmother filled a pint glass with Johnny Walker Blue and chugged it. Like a champion."

"Then what happened."

"Grandma was happy. The next morning she screamed at me in languages including, but not limited to, Korean and grunt."

"Why?"

"Maybe she was angry. She said, 'Mr. Lee! Sit down! Eat!' Everybody thought it was funny."

"Mr. Lee?"

"Apparently, Grandma was a handful. She disappeared regularly and nobody could find her. Eventually, some random person would bring her back. None of her evil kids were especially thrilled when she returned."

"Maybe she was a cunt," Wilson said, "but the language barrier made it difficult for you to tell."

"I wish I had a language barrier with my neighbors," I confessed to Wilson. "Those people are in the dictionary under cunts. I'm a big fan of dictionaries that have photos next to the occasional, seemingly-random, word."

"Why did your grandmother-in-law call you Mr. Lee?" the culturally ignorant man asked.

"She had a 33-percent chance of guessing correctly under normal Korean circumstances. The only other two surnames in South Korea, by law, are Kim and Park."

"Are you on drugs again?"

"Am I awake? If so, there's a 99 percent chance I am utilizing the tools mind-altering chemicals provide. I can only imagine the misery walking through life sans narcotics must be like."

"That's not a lot of people, according to the cartel."

"My neighbors need drugs."

"Your parents had to be on drugs when you were conceived. You have more visible birth defects than a five-legged goat."

"I have the low-dose Thalidomide to thank for many things."

"With all of your brain damage, I'm surprised you didn't end up being a cop."

"I know, that's the path most of us chose. The medical professionals consider me an outlier."

"Have you ever figured out why some people call the ground 'the floor' when referring to the surface underneath their feet outdoors?" Wilson asked.

"They're old school."

"What the hell does that mean?" Wilson asked.

"People who use the term, 'old school,' are people who never went to school."

"Do you think those people are happier than we are?"

"Of course they are. They're too stupid to figure out their government jobs are of no value to anyone on the planet."

"Does the chief have a government job?"

"He is the government."

"Do you think he's planning to use the recording studio we're building as a jail?"

"I don't know if you noticed, Micronesia is a toilet. Shoes were only recently discovered by the people of Chuuk."

"Same thing with the VCR."

"We must look like time travelers to those island hoppers."

"I'm glad you didn't use a different term for our Pohnpeian friends."

"The three-syllable word that starts with spear?"

TWENTY-THREE

PLAN A
STUDIO PLAN

PASADENA

T HE GANG FROM THE SPECIAL PROJECTS UNIT consulted with a man whose extensive knowledge of recording studios impressed us. "Honker Studios needs a floor that moves. It needs to bounce. Ballet doesn't happen on concrete," David Lee Roth said.

"What about IV7XI Studios?" I asked.

"Same thing in there but more," Dave responded. "Every night is ladies' night at IV7XI Studios. Come on down and get down."

"Freddie King is still going down, as far as I know," somebody said.

Most are unaware Dave always had a section of the plywood on the Van Halen stage designed to bounce like a trampoline. The man was and remains ahead of his time.

"Patrick, your girlfriend's back," Dave announced. "That's the good news."

"I'm not even asking—"

"The bad news is, your girlfriend's back."

"That was quick. I've heard the shelf life of a Tijuana hooker can be quite short."

"I hate to tell you this, Patrick," Dave said, "the Tijuana hooker career trajectory only lands with this kind of a *thud* when farm animals are involved."

"That only happens in Ensenada," I told Dave.

"I hate to tell you this Patrick…"

My phone rang and it was Wilson. "What's up CEO mofo?"

"Today is not a good day, man," I said.

"You should call Dave, he'll cheer you up."

"No, he won't. He just told me 7XI is back in town."

"That sounds like good news, Patrick," Wilson said.

"Dave also told me she's been fucking donkeys in Ensenada."

For a long time, the silence on the other end of the phone call felt like the setup for a punch line. "Felix fucks donkeys," Wilson said. What are the odds? I was the rare man with two acquaintances who knew everything about donkey dicks. "Did she suck donkey dicks?" Wilson had to ask.

"I suggest we approach this with empathy. 7XI may be ashamed of herself. Or, she may feel like a champion—not every teenager fucks a donkey."

"I'm guessing it's between two and three percent of teenagers," Wilson hypothesized.

"Instead of this back-and-forth maybe she did, maybe the donkey did, we should put together a list of questions."

Wilson started, "Tell me, 7XI, were you exclusive with one donkey or did every donkey in the stable get a piece of dat azz?"

"7XI, did you ever accidentally call a donkey Patrick in the heat of passion?"

Wilson had to go there, "7XI, what's it like to perform anilingus on a donkey?"

"Okay, I quit. Did I tell you we're going to Minneapolis next week?"

"Why?" Wilson asked.

TWENTY-FOUR

TARGET MEETS HONKER

MINNESOTA

"HOW THE FUCK DID THIS HAPPEN?"

"When you're on fire, people smell smoke, Wilson."

"That's a pretty good one. Your fire tornado jokes keep getting better and better. Shouldn't you be running a guitar company somewhere?"

"Your donkey fucker jokes need help. I sent everyone at the geriatric guitar company on vacation for an entire month and locked the doors of that godforsaken, lifeless, miseryland. We're using kung fu reverse business strategy to turn a Honda into a Maserati by creating a shortage of product. When we get back to work prices are double."

"That's a great idea," Wilson said. "Why are we going to Target?"

"Think about it. There's no reason a Rickenbacker should wholesale for less than five grand. Every single fucking guitar that leaves the building is a hand-crafted work of art. A masterpiece. It's Americana."

"Why the hell are we going to Target, again?"

"I just decided we're visiting the assholes at Target's corporate headquarters to sell them a company called Rickenbacker. Your name is now Wilson Rickenbacker."

"You're absolutely insane. Do you know what happens to people who piss off the Beatles?"

"As a matter of fact, I do. Jimmy Lamborghini shows up, finds some sucker to pay five times more than the company is worth and put him in charge, then he kills it and the entire industry. Fuck that guy."

"Good one," Wilson said. "For a second I thought you were gonna say the Eagles. Or Metallica. Same thing."

"We're visiting the garbage motherfuckers at Target because they're activating their Colorado Boulevard frontage as a result of the life we've breathed into the Route 66 scene. They're testing a bar/restaurant concept, adding a 10,000-square-foot elevated dining and drinking deck all the way across the front of the store, and testing a neighborhood market concept at street level. Target has seen what we've done and they want us to partner with them in some way."

"Does Chip know about this?"

"I don't know what Chip knows. After we hear what Target has to say we'll call him."

"My friend called me yesterday, he runs a fiesta company. He says we should do a Honker piñata."

"That's an automatic yes. We really do need to ask Chip for advice. We have so much going on, we need his help to prioritize our shit. Honker could be a multi-billion dollar licensing deal. Honker Burgers, Honker IPA, Honker Lube…"

"What about the Honkerbacker bass?"

"I have one."

"What if we add Honker departments in Target stores and replace the target in the Target logo with Honker?"

"We could die happy. Or we could do the right thing and tell those evil corporate cunts to eat shit and die."

"Why don't we propose the dumbest idea we can think of, make them give us a bunch of cash, and see if it works."

"What if it works?" I asked Wilson. "We don't want Target to make money."

"If it works we torpedo it."

"That's unethical," I said.

"We tell Target, 'We know this is a crazy idea. In the unlikely event it works, we're gonna torpedo it.' The Target fucks will laugh because they think we're making a joke. We never lie, we're upfront with our plan, impeccably ethical."

"Honker is more than a cartoon clown, he's my bro. We're not setting up Honker to fail. I'm telling them they need to paint all of their stores black, inside and out. Walmart is about to go with a deep, dark, gray. Paint it black."

Wilson was on drugs, so he had great ideas. "Let's propose an IV7XI boutique and only sell clothes for hookers and strippers. We give every item a name, like IKEA, but ours are in Spanish, and the IV7XI mascot is a smiling donkey."

"Do donkeys smile?"

"You haven't seen 7XI's videos, have you?"

<☒>

Wilson and I left our meeting with Target's ReachBiggerTeam with newfound knowledge—all of the biggest douchebags we'd been seeing around Minneapolis all those years worked at Target. The Target team's stupid questions pissed us off so we gave them *fuck you* answers that, from all indications, impressed the mediocre middle managers. We proposed a new concept, IV7XL, professional attire for large and lovely ladies who like to dress like hookers and strippers. With any luck the corporate creeps would leave us alone, we hoped.

I put on my EAD Logistics hat. "We've been too distracted with our crazy shit in Micronesia and Pasadena this year," I told Wilson. "We only have two small jobs in Arizona and New Mexico lined up for next year. Maybe something else in Minnesota and we still need to finish Chip's place. How are we making money next year?"

Wilson thought for a moment then told me in a hostile manner, "Blackwater."

"Awesome, problem solved."

"We bring them our billion-dollar idea."

I asked Wilson, "Which one?"

"Guitars for fat people."

Stunned and speechless I stared at Wilson like a fat person stares at the Sizzler salad bar.

"There are no guitars built to suit the needs of fatties," Wilson said.

"Are you suggesting vertical stripes to make the player appear thinner, or really heavy guitars so the player burns more calories, or gigantic guitars to obscure the view of the player's abdomen, or—"

"I don't know, I just pulled that out of my ass."

"That's what Felix said."

"As far as I can tell, all we need to do is tell people they look thinner and they buy shit," Wilson said. "It worked like a motherfucker for Richard Simmons."

I remained silent. He who doubteth the wisdom of Richard Simmons has no place in this world.

"Have you heard that Blowfly song, "Too Fat to—"

"Yes, a thousand times," I answered. "The priest at the church across the street from my friend's house in Los Gatos hated that song."

"Dave could be our guitars for fat people spokesman."

"Good idea. That Wolfgang guy is probably the fattest guitarist in rock 'n' roll right now."

"Does anybody know why he's so fat?"

"I'm sure Dave knows. If that guy ever stepped on the special plywood spot Dave used as a trampoline he would have fallen through the floor."

"Do you think Wolfgang flew across the stage on a wire like Michael Anthony?"

"Yes. Did Bill tell you about his trip to Africa with Dave?"

"Bill went to Africa with Dave?"

"When they got back from Africa Dave's guest house was gone. Bill just sent me a text and said Dave wants us to rebuild it for him."

"What happened to the last guest house?"

"1-800-GOT JUNK hauled it away."

"1-800-4-HONKER."

TWENTY-FIVE

HAPPY NEW YEAR!

SMILING HORSES

W E FOUND CHIP ON A COOL WINTER DAY AT AN AIRPORT, grateful for the ride and eager to see the scene he'd inspired and funded in Pasadena.

"Thank God. You motherfuckers are keeping me alive," said Chip as he sunk into the passenger seat of Wilson's gigantic he-man truck. "I spend all day with dickheads. Dickheads talking about internet bullshit."

"That internet bullshit has made you a billionaire, Chip," Wilson said.

"You get to hang out with Dave and Billthy Animal in California. I'm stuck with internet dickheads and accountants in Minnesota."

As we arrived at IV7XI/Honker, I pointed at the neighboring retail behemoth and told our hero, Chip, "Those Minnesota dickheads want to join our party."

Chip looked angry. "Target? Fuck those motherfuckers."

And that's how we secured our next $10 million investment from Blackwater. Apparently, everybody in Minnesota wanted to kill Target. Those Target cocksuckers are the most boring motherfuckers I've ever met, so call me if you need another executioner, Minneapolis.

We only had Chip for a minute before he needed to head for his hotel in Beverly Hills. "Things are about to explode with Blackwater," Chip said when we had a moment alone together in the secret cocaine room beneath the super-secret sub-basement of Honker Studios. "I have meetings with Apple, the Chinese, and Disney before Jimmy's New Year's Eve party."

"Lamborghini?"

"Yes."

"Never trust a guy named Jimmy."

While Chip was hobnobbing with knob gobblers in Beverly Hills we hosted the greatest New Year's Eve party Pasadena had ever seen. The beautiful sounds of live punk bands at incredibly high volume bounced off of tall buildings and long foreheads all over Pasadena for 12 hours until the silly horseback cops showed up and told us to turn it down. Why those horses looked at 7XI that way I will never know. A little band called Tropical Fuck Storm, operating on Australia time, woke up the fuckers camping out in front of our store waiting for the Rose Parade to start with a blistering indoor set on the IV7XI Records Stage at 4 a.m. Because we knew what the fuck we were doing, a film crew captured the Hendrix-at-

Woodstock wake-the-fuck-up event for posterity. If you haven't figured it out by now, I can't help you.

The rooftop fiesta wasn't the only party we had going. The all-night rave in IV7XI Studios turned into a topless foam party. The dungeon event in Honker Studios attracted registered sex offenders from near and far. Upstairs, Honker Records made the mistake of partnering with the dispensary next door for a reggae-themed party. IV7XI had parade campers outside fogging up our windows with steamy breath as Ivy and 7XI's first annual CalArts student stripper-a-thon fashion show raised money for underprivileged puppies and captivated the uninitiated.

Chip arrived just in time for the First Annual Honker Breakfast of Champions. The ever-responsible Dave insisted we stick to a strict schedule on New Year's Day. At 7:30 a.m. a breakfast of bacon, eggs, sausage, biscuits, gravy, whole milk, fresh fruit, oysters, bushmeat, champagne, orange juice, tequila, manchego cheese, special mushrooms, and coffee added the nutritional boost the cocaine lacked. At 8:15 a.m., 45 minutes before the scheduled start of the silly parade, we all retired to the basement's live room in Studio IV7XI for 20 minutes of feedback meditation. Let me tell you, there's nothing quite like lying on a floor in a pitch-black room with 20 of your closest friends while guitar amplifiers all over the place pointed in disparate directions fight feedback wars with each other.

Right after that and right before the parade arrived Tropical Fuck Storm hit the rooftop stage and launched into a blistering cover of "Unchained" prompting an overjoyed Dave to take over lead vocal duties and wind the crowd up down on the street. The highlight of highlights was the *Hey man, that suit is you!* part of the song Dave directed at one lucky parade goer who'll never forget that day.

When the parade started Dave and Tropical Fuck Storm hit Honker Studio One and worked on songs together. As the final float of the parade passed IV7XI/Honker the crowd failed to dissipate on our stretch of Colorado Boulevard, in fact, the opposite occurred. Word got out that Dave might perform after the parade. I wonder how we spread that rumor? Dave and Tropical Fuck Storm hit the stage and demolished the audience with a 50-minute long set of songs from Van Halen, Tropical Fuck Storm, Black Sabbath, David Bowie, AC/DC, Britney Spears, and more. Epic. All preserved for posterity by the film crew.

Chip was having difficulty processing the awesomeness, insanity, and debauchery observed before the clock struck noon. He told Wilson and I, "I just spent two days with every motherfucking CEO in the entertainment business. I heard the same bullshit I always hear out of their lame-ass mouths. Not a single new idea. Fuck those people! Whatever you maniacs are doing here is electric. What are we gonna do with it? Right now!"

"Let's go downstairs and grab a beverage in the IV7XIVIP Room," I suggested.

Wilson told Chip the story of Tropical Fuck Storm. I told Chip the story of the greatest man to ever walk the Earth, Peter Grant. Wilson told Chip about the footage our film crew captured of Tropical Fuck Storm from Australia to Micronesia to California. I wrapped everything up in a beautiful bow and told Chip, "You are Peter Grant, Tropical Fuck Storm are Led Zeppelin."

Without a second thought, Chip said, "Done." And, with that, Chip found a new lease on life.

*Honker recording vocals in Honker
Studios. Like a champion.*

The afterparty at Dave's place promised to be a humdinger. I was sick of talking to Wilson, especially after he asked me, "Is that crazy-ass record store recording studio place profitable?"

"It has to be," I answered. "Between Dave and those Kardashians down there in the studios we're bringing in $150,000 a month."

"Which Kardashians?"

"I have no idea. CPA Chris says everything's fine. By the way, I sold a bunker to Dr. Drew while Dave was screaming at the cops through his megaphone."

"Can this day get any weirder?" Wilson asked.

"Dave has a pet donkey around here somewhere."

By the end of the day, Chip bought a jet from Dave's attorney and told Ed he wanted us to build a runway for it at his house. Ed suggested he relocate permanently to Minnesota and handle business there exclusively, we agreed.

Taz called from Perth and said the rooftop fiesta with Tropical Fuck Storm and Dave was all over the television news in Australia. And he needed a doomsday bunker at his home in some kangaroo sanctuary there. We asked Hammer to handle that herself, she agreed, Tropical Fuck Storm was moving to Fremantle, anyway, so the stars aligned.

Liz headed off to Arizona to knock out a bunker for a baseball player. Bill told us Honker came to him in a dream and told him to open a Honker gas station in Pacoima. Ivy and 7XI invented their own language of animal noises en Español to communicate with each other. Somehow Robbo joined that cult.

Felix arrived late to the party in one of his typically bizarre fashion disasters—he always forgot one weird element when switching gender identities. Peggy convinced DD to go swimming in Dave's pool wearing a bikini several sizes too small. Wilson high-fived Peggy.

Because it was time for me to grow up and get a job, I told Wilson, "I don't want to do the doomsday bunker thing anymore. I need to focus on Rickenbacker full-time. The brand and the people deserve my undivided attention or I can't do it."

"That's what I would do," Wilson said. "Let's sell the Australian operation to Taz, help Ed find an investor to buy Minnesota, and find a buyer for Liz in the rest of America."

"Can we make the buyers hire us as consultants so we get three paychecks for almost zero work?" I asked.

"We can, but that would make us the same as police officers without the sexy uniforms."

"Will we get a discount at In-N-Out?"

"That woman still wants us to build her a bunker."

Before Chip left the party for the trip back to Minnesota I advised him, "Don't let your band go back to Australia. Keep 'em here, keep 'em busy, maintain momentum."

"Great idea, you handle it. Thank you for this incredible experience. I can't tell anybody about it—people won't believe me and they'll think I'm crazy."

"Yes, they will and won't."

Dave signaled my presence was required at his poolside gaggle. "Patrick, these Australians. What's their deal?"

"You saw it. They're 100 percent authentic. The best band on the fucking planet. On fire, motherfucking monsters."

"They're staying here," Dave said.

"I know. We're taking them to NAMM." NAMM is an acronym for the National Association of Music Merchants. Their annual trade show in Anaheim, California attracts people who give a shit about that shit and attracts people who want free shit.

"They should do a couple of shows locally before they own NAMM," Dave said.

"You read my mind, Dave. Rickenbacker rented out House of Blues in Anaheim for the whole week of the convention. It's the House of Tropical Fuck Storm, now."

"How did you guys make all this shit happen?"

"We just keep moving and do the stupidest shit we can think of every day, all day. Any sane person would have a thousand reasons to not do what we do."

"Bill wants to buy a gas station."

"Perfect example, Dave. We can't say no to that."

"What about the environmental impact?"

"We're doomed, we have 5 years left of this horseshit, at most, before the fires and floods and starvation and cannibalism kick in. We're fucked. That means we are unencumbered and can rock the casbah with absolute impunity."

"My neighbor says artificial intelligence will save us. You've probably heard of him—"

"Neil deGrasse Tyson is a bitch."

"Neil wants to go bicycle riding with me but I think he's probably a baby fucker."

"My approach to everything is follow instincts. My instincts are telling me to burn that fucker's house down."

"Tropical Fuck Storm brought fireworks."

I'd been hanging out with Tropical Fuck Storm all over the planet for months by then, but I'd been too intimidated to talk to any of them. Even Hammer. Because I was in awe of their majesty as a magical band. I didn't want to fuck that up.

"You have two superfans who are big shots in the music business who will do anything to see your band succeed. Taz is on your side, and me, too."

Tropical Fuck Storm frontman Gareth asked, "Who are you? I hear you're the donkey sucker's boyfriend."

"I don't know if all of that is true," I said to the blunt Australian guy. "I run Rickenbacker."

"How hard could that be? They haven't made anything new in my lifetime."

"Good point. It's my job to keep it that way. That's harder than anything. Every asshole thinks they have great ideas for everything."

"You're the wanker who started all this. Taz, Nagambie Speedway, Lauren, this trip," Gareth said. "I know who you are."

"What do you want to do?"

"We want to play live shows and record albums. If that's all we do, nothing else matters. We never stop, we all have other bands and solo projects, we do art, we want to do it all."

"The studios downstairs from the record stores are all yours, you're doing a couple of shows locally then a residency at House of Blues in Anaheim for a week during NAMM. February 1st you're in the studio with Dave producing the next Tropical Fuck Storm record. You're going on the road after that. Chip told me to make you the biggest band on the planet. Give me 18 months, man."

"We've heard all of that bullshit before."

"You get to live with David Lee Roth. Here, take this."

"How much money is this?"

"$50,000. United States dollars, not that bootleg Canadian thing you Australians use. You won't need to spend any of it on bullshit for the next 18 months. You're living here or on the road, everybody's on a salary, per diem, you'll sell records and T-shirts and tickets, we're serious."

"We're in, mate."

"Chip just texted me, he wants you guys in Minnesota this weekend for a barbecue. We'll fly in Friday, no need to bring much gear."

"Fuck yeah."

"Oh, you need a new drummer. Hammer wants to do construction in Perth. Talk to Dave."

Hungover, I went back to work at Rickenbacker the next day. They didn't need me there. I stayed in the hellish Orange County tilt-up industrial park unit designed to kill any will to live for a couple of days then flew with Tropical Fuck Storm to Duluth. Blackwater HQ, a charity event Chip hosted in St. Paul, a punk club in Minneapolis, and out. A couple of days later a show at the Smell, then The Troubadour in West Hollywood and off to NAMM for a week in Anaheim.

Tropical Fuck Storm owned the NAMM show in many ways. Chip's buddy Ron White agreed to MC Rickenbacker's House of Tropical Fuck Storm for the duration of the convention. A film crew followed Ron and Gareth around the convention floor on the first day while Gareth pretended to be Rickenbacker's president. The whole band charmed the convention floor by day and murdered the crowd at House of Blues by night.

By the end of the convention Tropical Fuck Storm were best friends with everyone in the musical instrument business, all members had signed multiple endorsement deals with gear manufacturers, and the band returned to Honker/IV7XI Studios with a truckload of free shit.

Even better news. At NAMM I met a guy working for a competitor in the booth next to Rickenbacker's. His name was Gary. I don't trust people named Gary, they're almost always child molesters, but this guy was different.

"What's it like working for Gibster?" I asked Gary.

"Gibster is okay. I fucking hate Nashville, but I hate Los Angeles even more," Gary said.

"Do you like this neighborhood?" I asked.

"Yeah, I drove down the street yesterday and ran into a beach. A fucking beach! I would kill to live here."

"Let's go. We're going to the Library."

A mile or so through the elephant-sized herd pile known as Anaheim, California we arrive at our destination.

Gary was confused, "This place is a library?"

"No, it's *The* Library."

Over chicken wings, burgers, and tequila with Anaheim's finest strippers, our happy hours at The Library Gentlemen's Club convinced me Gary was the right man to lead Rickenbacker while I assisted with Tropical Fuck Storm's path to international superstardom.

"Gary, you're Rickenbacker's COO effective right now."

"Yes, I am, Patrick. Yes, I am."

Gareth showed up and we hatched a plan to fuck with Gary's former employer the next day. Gary couldn't help himself—he called his boss from the VIP room and said. "Fuck you! I quit!!" In the morning his former colleagues were surprised to see a happy Gary working the Rickenbacker booth like a champion. Gary's first act as COO was to announce Rickenbacker would no longer sell products through Blackwater. A brilliant move, Chip thought it was a master stroke—we didn't have anything to sell, anyway.

One day at the studio between takes, Gareth said, "Patrick, we want one of these big houses we see around here. We saw one near Huntington Gardens we like. When can we get one of those?"

"What time is it?" I asked Gareth. "If that's what you want, that's the goal we work towards. Let's go to Jumbo's and put together a plan."

The plan was to put all the money from record sales, live shows, endorsement deals, and merch in the bank. Blackwater pays all expenses, none of which are recoupable.

"How do you get paid?" Gareth asked.

"I'm an equal partner in Tropical Fuck Storm. You four and me. 20% each. Just like Led Zeppelin and Peter Grant. You're Led Zeppelin."

"Did Led Zeppelin make more money than Van Halen?"

"Twenty times."

"Do we get an airplane with a fireplace like Led Zeppelin?"

"Do you want castles or an airplane?"

"Yes."

"We're bringing the movie crew back for a couple of weeks in Europe then we edit and submit the movie to next year's film festivals. Keep sending those guys everything you shoot. Taz is still funding that. He'll be here for the record launch."

"Are we using his pressing plant?"

"We're using every pressing plant. It's our label, I'll have a worldwide distribution deal in place this week for the first record. Let's go see Wilson."

On the way from Jumbo's to Wilson's house Chip called.

"Dave changed the name of his band."

"Dave Halen?" Gareth asked.

"Hello, Australia! Patrick, Dave's band is now Dave y Los Daves. Everybody in the band is named Dave, now. Dave Tuba, Dave Trombone, it's hilarious. He wants everybody in the band to do a solo album. You're in charge of Blackwater Records now, see ya later!"

"That's epic," Gareth said.

"If I'm in charge I'm changing the name of the record company," I told Gareth.

"What's the new name?" he asked.

"It will appear when we least expect it. Let's go see Carlito Bandito. Wilson is no fun."

TWENTY-SIX

CARLITO'S MEAN CHORDS

LOS ANGELES

*Z*APPA HAD THE GREATEST MUSTACHE EVER. Geezer tried, we all tried, however, nobody came close.

"Who's a bitch?" I asked Carlito Bandito.

"You're a bitch."

"Wrong answer."

"Neil."

"Neil who?

"Neil deGrasse Tyson's a bitch," Carlito said. "Excuse me, the tree phone's ringing."

Carlito Bandito returned from his tree phone conversation and told me, "I don't wanna be in your band."

"I didn't fucking ask you to be in my band, asshole. You're a shitty guitar player, C.C. I'm here to buy drugs."

"Your chords aren't mean enough. I need mean chords, man. Really fucking mean."

Gareth was pretending to be my deaf cousin. We gave Carlito a Tropical Fuck Storm T-shirt and told Carlito it was Gareth's band. Carlito asked, "How can a deaf guy be in a band?"

I said, "He's a lip reader." Gareth and I laughed hysterically, Carlito was angry.

"Get out!"

"Carlito, fuck you. What's your problem? I paid for your mom's abortion. Thanks for the drugs. I'll be back. And I'll be armed. Armed with mean chords. You motherfucker."

"Carlito Bandito," Gareth said as we walked back to the car.

"Yeah, what about him," I asked.

"Carlito Bandito Records."

"See, it appeared. Let's go see Jimmy."

Jimmy was one of those record business cunts who believed everybody in the business who ever tasted a tiny little slice of success owed a debt of gratitude to Jimmy's Malibu real estate fund. What a cunt. I hated that little bitch, so we went to his office.

"Fuck you, Jimmy."

"I don't think you know who you're talking to."

"Fuck you. I know exactly who I'm talking to, Jimmy. Fuck you."

"Be real careful here, young man," Jimmy said.

"What the fuck is wrong with you?" I asked Jimmy.

"I'm the motherfucker who made you rich."

"No, you're not. You're the motherfucker who needs to shut the fuck up and suck my cock."

"Or what?"

"Have you ever seen one of these?"

Jimmy asked, "A gun?" right before chunks of Jimmy Lamborghini's brain, skull and scalp flew out of the exploding window behind his desk.

Shit, I thought to myself. *Wrong Jimmy.*

"Is that legal in America?" Gareth asked.

"What?"

"Murder."

"More or less. I'd consider that self-defense. Jimmy Lamborghini murdered the whole music business. Millions of people lost jobs. Families starved. I did that, we did that, for the children."

"His children must be assholes."

"There is no doubt those little shits are cunts. Anybody who grows up owning four miles of the beach in Southern California is a stupid cunt," I informed Gareth. "A lot of people say Jimmy Lamborghini's kids rape babies. And it runs in the family."

Gareth asked me a serious question. "Do you know who Jimmy's baby-raping kids' favorite band was?"

"No, I wish I did."

"U2?"

TWENTY-SEVEN

SANDWICH OF LOVE

LOS ANGELES

A FTER A LONG DAY MURDERING PEOPLE, all I wanted was a sandwich and some sleep. *Fuck this* I thought to myself. *This is all bullshit, I don't want to live on this fucking planet one more minute.*

"Are you here?" a wispy voice from the basement asked.

That's a stupid question. I'm not answering that. I was hungry so I started making a sandwich.

"Are you here?"

What the fuck? "Stop asking stupid questions and come make me a sandwich."

"I don't know how."

I don't talk to people or ghosts or whatever who don't know how to make sandwiches, so I shut the door to the subterranean dungeon and went to bed with a sandwich in my hand.

During a dream where I was managing a record store with a trackless roller coaster flying through walls, ceilings, and floors as Billthy Animal led an aerobics class full of farm animals in the upside-down swimming pool, I was rousted by an angry, almost-feminine, voice screaming, "You motherfucker!"

A split-second before 7XI's Rickenbacker bass would have met my skull I rolled off of the bed and grabbed my Glock. I knew it was 7XI, but I pulled the trigger a couple of times, anyway. Amazingly the cops believed me when I told them I found her dead. I showed the dimwit detectives PornHub videos from Ensenada and YouTube videos of 7XI ballin' with her pimp in Dave's stolen car and cried a lot.

For a minute I was upset 7XI was dead and her pimp was on wanted lists. Then I looked at census figures and learned there were more than 7 million women between the ages of 18 and 20 in the United States. What are the odds?

PART 4
HIGHER EDUCATION

TWENTY-EIGHT

ANGRY FROM THE HEAT

TROPICAL FUCK STORM ROARED OUT OF THE STUDIO in it to win it and out for blood. *Anger Ranger* captured the band in all its maniacal glory. David Lee Roth saw what the band was capable of, set the table, lit it on fire, and took a chainsaw to it. Dave hit the road south of the border with his spectacular band of muchachos while Tropical Fuck Storm embarked on a month-long coast-to-coast record release party to set up the forthcoming album.

Boston was the first city, an acoustic show in Cambridge Square and a club gig in a shitty part of Boston. It's a college town. The band used a day off to film a video for "Filthy Girl" in a half-demolished factory dressed in yellow jumpsuits like DEVO. Robotic movements clashed with the music, but it worked like a charm.

Next Brooklyn, Jersey, Philadelphia, then back to Brooklyn. The first of two videos Dave directed landed between the Brooklyn shows and we saw a noticeable increase in interest at the second show. Word was getting around.

Miami wasn't ready for Tropical Fuck Storm; the bad press and worse behavior of the band's antics in Florida generated something. A three-day bombardment of Nashville left a lasting impression. Chicago didn't care. Ann Arbor and Madison pissed off pissed off college kids. The day the record landed in stores Tropical Fuck Storm returned to Minnesota as champions, destroying the team at Blackwater and then mutilating Minneapolis. Chip was around but seemed distracted.

From Minneapolis through our three-day invasion of Los Angeles, a few journalist-types followed us around and fell under the band's spell. We bid adieu to the United States with a farewell show on the rooftop of Honker/IVRIP that felt like the end of a chapter to some. The crew in the stores, the band, and the rest of us gathered afterward in the bus at Barney's Beanery amazed at what we had done and seen, but somehow subdued. Maybe we were tired.

A few days terrorizing London bookended by tiny club shows preceded a two-week run all over the British Isles, culminating in a final show at Hammersmith Odeon. We hit as many clubs in Scandinavia as we could before the

European festival circuit kicked off. Then back to North America and 28 club shows in 40 days starting in Toronto.

Chip had been uncharacteristically unresponsive to our communications for a while, so it didn't come as a big surprise when CPA Chris called and said, "Patrick, Blackwater has been sold to a private equity firm and they say they won't be paying any of the bills I've sent them."

CPA Chris and Bill in less complicated times.

"What bills are those?"

"I've been sending them bills for all kinds of things and they've paid 'em all. You guys are rich!"

"Don't tell anyone. Let me figure this out. Anything else?"

"Dave's record is selling like crazy. That was really smart to set up the record company so you owned it."

"I know."

"Oh, almost forgot. Go get your movie. All of the film, the hard drives, everything. Do that now. Take it to Frank's place, he has climate-controlled storage. I'll text you the address. Go now."

I called Gareth. "G-man, we need to go on a secret mission."

In the car on the way to the shithole known as the San Fernando Valley, I told my passenger, "Gareth, I think our world is about to collapse all around us."

"Don't worry, mate, it happens all the time."

"We're picking up your movie and stashing it at Frank's."

"Who's Frank?"

"I don't know."

"Perfect."

Like that time I had full access to Diplo's offices in the former Beastie Boys/Grand Royal space in Atwater Village, the production company's offices were empty and the doors unlocked so we grabbed our intellectual property, a box of office supplies, the petty cash drawer, and a few expensive cameras on our way out.

"Don't you think they have cameras in there?" Gareth asked.

"Not so much anymore. We're headed downtown to Frank's."

The address CPA Chris texted me led us to a cold storage facility near Little Tokyo. We walked inside and the place smelled like frozen disappointment.

"Hi, we're here to see Frank," I said.

"Frank's dead."

"Is Frank Jr. here?"

"Frank Jr. died before Frank."

Gareth was angry and asked, "Who the fuck is in charge, then, you freeze-dried fuckhead?"

Some guy in a Member's Only jacket said, "I like 'dis guy," and we were in the cold storage posse.

Frank turned out to be Frank Sinatra. Frank owned a beer distribution company at one time and kept his most important shit in a cold storage vault protected by his posse. Films, masters of his recordings, trophies, cars, all kinds of everything. Gareth and I left there knowing we would never see our shit again without giving the mob a slice. Allegedly.

"Gareth, can you keep a secret?"

"Not really."

"I've killed 35 fewer people this year than Wilson killed last year."

"I know, I was there."

"You were there when I killed 7XI?"

"We all were. 7XI did a donkey show in your basement every Wednesday night. A different donkey every week."

"You're telling me, 7XI cheated on me with dozens of donkeys?"

"That's crazy talk. I think it was hundreds. She was doing at least four shows every week and she demanded fresh meat, if you know what I mean. I know you don't want to hear this, but, after a few shows, I couldn't miss one."

"Why?"

"You never knew who the donkey was in advance. When the donkey arrived your mind always went to the, 'Oh, no, this won't end well,' zone."

"Thank you, goodnight."

"Every donkey had a weird and wildly unique penis."

"Great, I've heard it all now."

"Then there were the noises—"

All I could do to stop the conversation was break out my sonic secret weapon—the first Mercyful Fate EP. I didn't need to hear any more details of my dead teenage girlfriend's donkey fucking. Or the donkey anilingus. "I'm not Neil deGrasse Tyson," I told Gareth, "leave me out of this bullshit."

TWENTY-NINE

THE SEVERED HEAD

ALL THE SIGNS AND SYMPTOMS FLASHED AND ACHED, however, we chose not to believe what we saw with our very own eyes and felt within our genitals. Until we couldn't. The recording studios started to hear *no* from gear wrangler Colton at Blackwater. Dave was on the road with his 20-piece band when the Blackwater credit card stopped working. And then there were the raids. The dirty pigs raided the studios, the record stores, my house, Wilson's house, and Dave's house the same day. Government employees aren't very good at raiding places or doing anything else. I'm pretty sure the dogs FBI agents bring to raids are emotional support puppies. Not once have any one of those silly dogs found my ample drug stash.

In my infinite wisdom, I found my way to Dave's house where news people assembled. I related how lucky the pig people were their tanks missed Australia's greatest band, Tropical Fuck Storm, who, only a day earlier, were in rehearsals for their tour in support of the new album, *Anger Ranger*, in stores now. Unaware of the tragedy, I told the microphone-wielding robots, "Neil deGrasse Tyson says *Anger Ranger* will save the world from climate change."

"Neil deGrasse Tyson is a bitch," said the dude leaning against the wall of Dave's compound wearing sunglasses at night.

I stared at the rude dude heckling me, there was something about the guy I couldn't quite figure out.

"It's Carlito Bandito, your drug dealer."

Carlito's timing was, as usual, impeccable. The way the news station reported the story was, "Breaking news at 11, *it's Carlito Bandito, your drug dealer*, America's greatest living scientist, Neil deGrasse Tyson, found dead in Mexico. Federal agents raid singer David Lee Roth's home searching for evidence. Cindy Suzuki has the latest from Pasadena..." Dave finished signing autographs and posing for photos with the garbage Uvalde people, then he led the Bandito and yours truly into the compound for a beach barbecue.

"Why did the cops raid all of our houses, Dave?" I asked.

"A decapitated Neil deGrasse Tyson was found in Ensenada wearing a Tropical Fuck Storm T-shirt with 7XI's phone number in his pocket," Dave said. "Who's this guy?" Dave asked about Carlito Bandito.

"I'll yell ya later," I answered.

Dave continued, "A stray dog ran through the crime scene, grabbed Neil deGrasse Tyson's severed head by the tongue, and ran away with it."

I told Dave, "I can see that image in my mind clear as day."

"Eyes wide open," Dave said.

"Yes. Eyes wide open. The pigs who raided my place stole the pizza I'd just had delivered."

"That's fucked up. I gotta tell ya, Patricio Negro, we need to write a song about the true story of Neil deGrasse Tyson giving head to a dog."

"And then another one about the dog giving head to a bunch of cops when the pigs find the dog," Carlito said.

"That's a good idea. Carlito Bandito is a guitar scientist," I told Dave.

"Carlito, if Patricio Negro is correct, and he has never steered me wrong, you're in the band."

Like Freddie King, Carlito wasted no time sticking his big feet out the window and his head on the ground, or something like that, "Neil deGrasse Tyson gives cabeza to un perra fea."

"I think I have a uniform in your size," Dave told Carlito. "You might be in two bands, now. Can you drive a bus?"

I left Dave and Carlito alone to hammer out details of whatever the planet had in store for us. I called Wilson's landline to see if his house was still standing.

"You motherfucker," Peggy answered.

"Do you kiss Felicia with that mouth?"

"Fuck you, Patrick. Fuck you. Wilson is in jail on $1 million bond. The feds found a turkey fryer, invoices for air purification systems, and blueprints for secret underground laboratories. He's facing life in prison."

"Peggy, that's preposterous, you know we would never be involved in that kind of monkey business."

"No, I don't. I was in Palm Desert. The feds found Wilson, DD, and Felix in bed together. What do you think's going on there?"

"I don't know, I don't even want to know. If it makes you feel any better, 7XI was fucking donkeys in Ensenada."

Wilson booking photo/online dating avatar.

"What's that on the grill?" Carlito asked.

Dave replied, "We're having tako hot dogs, young man. Save some room, you're headed to outer space."

Carlito knew what Dave was telling him. "I've had meatball tacos at Sizzler before."

"Take a King's Hawaiian hot dog bun, sake marinated octopus arm grilled to perfection, Dave's Squid Ink Ghost Pepper Sauce, Japanese mayo, fermented and shredded taro, bonito flakes, crispy garlic chips, boom."

"Octopus arm?" Carlito exclaimed.

Peggy sent me a text message. "Oh, no. Wilson's headed to the SuperMax," I announced.

"Great. Tell him we need regular hot dogs," Carlito said.

"The federal prison, not the supermarket," I told Carlito. "He'll be okay unless he talks about the fire tornado."

"We don't talk about fire tornados, motherfucker," the hangry Carlito said.

"Dave y los Tornados de Fuego," said the wise man holding down the barbecue fort.

At that very moment, lightning struck a tree on Dave's neighbor Neil deGrasse Tyson's property signaling approval from above for Dave and Carlito's new project. Dave and Carlito entered Honker Studios and didn't come out until their debut album *Cabeza* was complete.

Taz pressed *Cabeza* in his Aussie rock 'n' roll factory, Dave y los Tornados de Fuego hit the ground in Taztown and joined Tropical Fuck Storm on a triumphant, conquering, blitzkrieg of every single city and town ready to rock. Australia. New Zealand, Japan, and some places we can never talk about fell under the thunder of that which only the survivors of the Dave y los Tornados de Fuego and Tropical Fuck Storm double-bill can speak of.

After the final Tokyo show we all retreated to Dave's dojo in the foothills of Mount Fuji to regenerate for a week. Carlito brought his own gourmet gas station cuisine.

"Patrick, we need to take Tropical Fuck Storm to Sinaloa," Dave said. "Sinaloa is the next Ibiza." I didn't tell Dave there was no fucking way we were ever going to Sinaloa.

The Tropical Fuck Storm/Fire Tornado express next landed in the spiritual homeland of Tropical Fuck Storm, Pohnpei. Virtually every resident of Pohnpei had a personal connection to Tropical Fuck Storm based on the time the band spent touring the entire island getting to know the Pohnpeians last time they were there. Tropical Fuck Storm fans lined the sides of the runway at the airport as our plane landed. As the plane slowed to a halt, emergency evacuation devices deployed. The band members slid down the inflated death traps into the open arms of weeping fans. Carlito Bandito went face-first. Dave stood at the top of the slide nodding his approval and admiration. He looked at me and said, "Fuck, yeah."

Fuck, yeah, indeed. Our invading army of rock 'n' roll saviors assembled on Taz Mountain for, you guessed it, a barbecue. Taz told me, "I watched that whole fucking thing at the airport with my drone. It was like watching the fall of Saigon in reverse."

"You should've been at the show in Ho Chi Minh City," I told Taz.

"Every kid on this island is in a band. So are most of the adults. None of 'em sound the same and none of 'em sound like Tropical Fuck Storm. It's absolutely mental," Taz said.

"Wait until you see Dave's band. We have a container of tubas, trumpets, trombones, saxophones, accordions, and guitars being unloaded at the port right now."

"Accordions? God help us all."

Taz was in hiding on Pohnpei, so he missed all of the shows we'd done in Australia and elsewhere.

"I like Dave's record, and I saw some of the live footage on TikTok, who's in the band?"

"Dave, Carlito Bandito, Dave Tuba, Dave Drums, Dave Saxophone, Dave Trombone, Dave Trumpet…"

"Who plays the accordion?"

"Carlito Bandito's sister."

"The way Carlito Bandito leaps on stage, Carlito must be getting all the pussy."

"That's what I thought would happen, too. Believe it or not, we're both wrong. Totally wrong. The tuba guy gets all the pussy. It's weird."

Early the next morning, Dave y los Tornados de Fuego and Tropical Fuck Storm set off on independent goodwill tours of Pohnpei, Dave's band on a counter-clockwise orientation, Tropical Fuck Storm in a clockwise direction. Every town and village and school awaited the legends' arrival with a battle of the bands and a massive barbecue. The two bands met in Nan Madol for an audience with the chief, whose appearance resplendent in the most amazing of tribal attire—a badass, bespoke Tropical Fuck Storm aloha shirt— awed us all.

"Welcome back, motherfuckers. I hope you can top last time," the chief said.

"What was the highlight last time?" I asked the chief.

"The encore, 'For Those About to Rock.' Every man, woman, and child on Pohnpei wakes up singing that song in the morning."

I just nodded. Pohnpei wasn't ready for the Tropical Fuck Storm/Dave/Carlito version of "Unchained."

Dave told the chief, "Hey man, that shirt is *you*!"

Pohnpei lived and breathed nothing but Tropical Fuck Storm and Dave y los Tornados de Fuego for as long as they could take it; we all got leid and departed the island paradise with a vow to return.

The traveling circus next introduced its unique brand of multicultural rock to the Hawaiian Islands, returned to North America for 6 weeks of shows, traveled across the Atlantic for a couple of months of awesomeness, and then took a well-deserved break at Dave's estate in Southern Portugal. After a few days, Dave, Carlito, and Gareth departed for Spain to buy flamenco guitars, the rest of the Daves flew back to Sinaloa, leaving me alone with the ladies of Tropical Fuck Storm. I learned being a sex slave is not all it's cracked up to be after the first day or so. And, a couple of days after that, the romantic flamenco sound of a nylon-stringed acoustic guitar gets old real fast.

None of us wanted to leave Portugal and its amazing hashish, but some of us had court dates scheduled in California.

THIRTY
BROCK GETS CLOCKED
THE DAM

B ACK AT HOME IN LOS ANGELES, I wanted to take some time off, but I remembered a quote from a wise man: "The people who are trying to make this world worse aren't taking a day off. How can I?" Exactly, Bob Marley, evil never sleeps. Let's go see Bill and find out who's fucking with us and make a plan to destroy the evil motherfucker.

"Stephanie's boyfriend," Bill said over drinks at the Honker Records commissary, Barney's Beanery. "Brock."

"Did you say something?" I asked Bill.

"See what I mean. That rack is like a tractor beam teleporting your eyeballs into an alien spaceship. Brock shows up here in his business/casual long-sleeved shirt tucked into his pants, grabs a pool stick, and glowers at me staring at his girlfriend. I really don't appreciate that."

"What? Growlers?"

"Brock is another one of those backward baseball cap, flip-flop, cargo short people who need cock down their throats as often as I need tequila and cocaine," Bill said. "Stephanie complains a lot about him. Did we miss the day in school when we were supposed to learn about this shit?"

"Probably. We didn't go to Catholic school or USC," I explained to Bill.

"University of Sucking Cock?"

"Did you say something?"

So, we hatched a plan to kill the bastard named Brock. Bill told Brock about the new electric bicycle department at Honker Records, then Bill gave Brock an amazing discount on a Pedego Trail Tracker fat bike. Somehow the electric bicycle sensed when Brock was riding across Devil's Gate Dam and sent Brock airborne in a way that so impressed NASA engineers from Jet Propulsion Laboratory gathered for a team-building picnic lunch nearby they vowed to name the next rocket launch mission designed to slam into an asteroid, Brock. Goodbye, Brock, enjoy knitting socks that smell.

Bill and I observed Brock's demise from a nearby, clandestine location. We were quite pleased with our work. "Maybe we should do this for a living," Bill proposed.

"Do what?" I asked.

"Kill people," he said. "That was really fun. And I think we're really good at it."

"I'm not convinced that's a solid business, Bill. It didn't earn us any money."

Bill concurred. "You're right. It's probably a better hobby than a vocation."

"Hey, don't get me wrong, I'm all about sending assholes and motherfuckers into the afterlife all day every day. Who's next?"

Bill's pragmatism convinced me he was growing and maturing as a human being. "Let's set up a murder calendar. You know me, I wanna kill all day, every day, however, a disciplined approach is the way to approach this unless you want to hang out with Wilson in the SHU."

"What the hell is the shoe?" I asked.

The SHU—*S, H, U*. It stands for Special Housing Unit. Solitary confinement."

"What's so bad about solitary confinement in prison? Do prisoners miss hanging out with other prisoners? I've always wondered why people in prison would complain about that."

THIRTY-ONE

THE MYSTERY OF DD WHITE

XXX

O N THE WAY FROM SUSHI TO THE ICE HOUSE TO SEE RON WHITE, DD said, "I need a massage," as she twisted that thing around on the top of her neck.

I said, "I need a prostate massage."

To which DD responded, "Oooh, I need to practice, my final exam is coming up. I'm taking a class in that."

"What school is that?"

"I'm being home-schooled at my teacher's house."

"Taylor Swift was home-schooled."

"Don't tell me that, Patrick! Taylor practiced guitar four hours every day, six on the weekends."

"I'm free all weekend."

DD and I spent a few minutes talking to Ron after his remarkable performance. When DD excused herself to handle business in the ladies' room, Ron asked, "What's the story with this one? She's dynamite."

"She's studying massage and she needs practice. What are you doing Sunday?"

Bill and some unidentified guy at The Ice House. Two-drink minimum strictly enforced.

"Nothing. Let's have a barbecue."

"No. I'm sending DD over to practice her massage technique. Her final exam is Monday, she's nervous."

DD left my house Sunday morning and I never saw her again. Ron and I never mentioned her again. On stage, in subsequent years, Ron had that far-away stare PTSD provides and his set included many new topics most of his audience failed to appreciate such as rusty trombone and Tony Danza. Tony Danza the verb, not Tony Danza the noun.

Back at Barney's Beanery a few days later, Bill said, "Sorry to hear about DD. Do you miss her or 7XI more?"

"7XI was ridonkulous."

"How long have you been waiting to use that one?"

"A long time. Donkey years."

"I hear 7XI works for Sammy in Cabo San Lucas."

"Sammy invented mountain biking."

"I know. I sell mountain bikes."

"I wonder if Sammy has an electric mountain bike?"

Ultimately, we decided Sammy wasn't worth the effort.

"Bill, when we were told life would be so goddamned crazy? When I was a kid, the expectation was: go to school, get a job, meet a woman, then most of your decisions in life were made, time to watch TV."

"Patrick, you stupid cunt. We chose to live this way because any other way is fucking bullshit."

"I don't remember making that decision. Was there a box on my driver license application, or something?"

THIRTY-TWO
CONRAD UNIVERSITY
CALIFORNIA

ONE DAY MY PHONE RANG, it was none other than the long-lost Chip Conrad.

"Chip! It's been years!"

"Donkey years," Chip said. "I'm in Anaheim for NAMM next week. Are you around?"

"Yes! What are you doing at NAMM?"

"I don't know, my non-compete agreement with the cunts who bought Blackwater just expired, trying to figure out what to do next."

"Do you want to stay at Dave's? He's out of town."

"No, we need a whole new scene for chapter two. Meet me at my hotel in Huntington Beach."

Chip's hotel across the highway from the beach featured one of those B-list celebrity dining/entertainment establishments so popular in tourist trap locales from coast to fucking coast. I sat down on its ocean-view patio, ordered a half-dozen margaritas made from the tequila brand the restaurant's owner started with doppelgänger Guy Ferrari, shoved rocks of cocaine into my nose regardless of who might see, and thought the same thing I did every day growing up in Orange County attending Huntington Beach's Ocean View High School: *I want to kill myself.*

Chip arrived and said, "I didn't know your girlfriend worked at Sammy's restaurant in Huntington Beach."

"Yeah…"

"What are the odds?"

"Yeah…"

"Patrick, you look like I did the first year after I sold Blackwater—lost. Enjoy it while it lasts. We're about to stir some things up."

Chip was rested, reenergized, and ready to attack the next chapter of his life with gusto. "What do you propose we do next, Patrick?"

"I don't know, Chip. I have a feeling we won't find that out at NAMM, either, but we need to go there anyway."

"I'm looking forward to NAMM. We don't have any business meetings scheduled but we're hanging out with my old friends all day, every day. We don't need to worry about seeing anything, we get to listen and learn. We leave here in an hour to meet Toshi for dinner."

Oh, boy. Chip might not know about the last time I saw Toshi. Samurai-wielding maniacs later identified as Carlito

Bandito and Toshi destroyed a suite in the Tokyo hotel Frank Lloyd Wright designed. Talk about expensive furnishings...

"Where are we?" Chip asked as the limousine Toshi sent for us drove down mile after mile of streets lined with bombed-out industrial buildings.

"Gardena. This is where the real Japanese food in America is."

The micro restaurant Toshi invited us to seated about twenty. Our party of six, a table for two a young couple occupied, and a table of twelve where none other than a heavily disguised man known as David Lee Roth was holding court in an uncharacteristically low-key manner.

Chip gave me a wide-eyed, what the fuck look, I said, "Yeah..." The *welcome to my world* part was unspoken yet understood.

Over dinner, little was mentioned about the music industry. Chip talked about his recent experiences fishing all over Minnesota, and Toshi filled us in on the latest fads in Japanese culture. My uninitiated and ill-informed opinion of Japanese youth culture is they are into things twenty years old or twenty years in the future. The virtual reality headset hacky sack craze combined both, I figured.

We didn't intrude upon Dave's fiesta, on his way out the door he turned toward me and mouthed, *you're a fucking winner, man,* and stepped back out into the real world like a champion in action.

NAMM was fun, yet uninspiring, in a direct sense. "What did you learn?" Chip asked.

"I learned nobody knows what's happening. These are people who live and die by their ability to spot trends, nobody has a clue what's on the horizon. The smart people we talked to were hungry to learn. Not learn about the next big thing, but learn about real shit. I did learn the only thing to do is run as fast as you can away from anybody talking about artificial intelligence like it's a good thing."

Chip thought about what I had said and asked, "What do we do next?"

"Okay, I've been thinking about this and I have an idea. I propose we pick six places to visit for three days each. We land, we look, we listen, we learn. We don't go where trends are supposed to be born. Six places, all different from each other, the last places one would ever go to find the next big thing. And we don't look for it. We live and learn."

"Okay, where are we going tomorrow?"

"Yerevan."

"No."

"Warsaw."

"Okay."

"747, business class?"

'Yes!"

"Perfect, we're leaving for LAX in an hour."

Ultimately, we didn't go anywhere other than Europe and we came back after Warsaw, Munich, Stockholm, and Madrid.

"Chip, here's my idea: we start a school where we teach people what they want to learn. One class per semester. The class is determined by written requests submitted by potential students. It could be about anything."

"That's a good way to learn what people want to learn."

"I think so. We pick the best idea, and interview the person or people with that idea, along with the student or students who presented the idea we figure out who we want to teach the class, and the instructor works with said student or students to develop the curriculum. and they invite a dozen or so other students who might be interested. Those pay very little, we sell tickets to others to fill the room."

"I like it. A core group of students will be heavily invested, others will pay admission. Do we need to get accredited or offer degrees?"

"Nope, nobody cares about that shit anymore."

"Where do we do it?"

"Duluth."

Our approach to marketing and operating the school involved no email, social media, or online advertising. We hired a few people to blanket Duluth with flyers and posters with a post office box for correspondence. The first two weeks we didn't see a single response. On my way to meet Chip for happy hour one day, I walked into our UPS store to look at our empty mailbox. The guy running the place asked, "Do you run some kind of school or something?"

"Not for long."

"Here, these keep showing up, you must be giving out the wrong box number." UPS Store guy handed me a stack of 56 cards and letters.

Chip was in our usual booth at the sports bar scrolling through bullshit on his phone. He didn't look happy. I dropped the cards and letters on the table and we shared a good laugh. A few class suggestions were of a sexual nature, a surprising number were criminal activities, and relationship-type classes were suggested. Three were sincere requests for real-world information about starting a business. We decided that would be the perfect class to start with. We called the three people who submitted the request, they all joined us for happy hour, by the end of the evening the entire deal was set.

"That was easy," I told Chip.

"I can't believe how much fun this is already," Chip replied.

With Duluth set, I headed back home and used our Duluth blueprint to set something similar up in Pasadena.

THIRTY-THREE

COLD-BLOODED KILLERS

LOS ANGELES

C HIP WAS HAPPY, THAT'S ALL THAT MATTERED. Back in Los Angeles, I instantly lost interest in the crazy school project and thought for a minute about what I really enjoyed doing most: killing people. Seeing that asshole, Brock, die left me with a sense of deep satisfaction. There wasn't any one person I needed to kill, so I made a list of a few people I disliked and ranked them in terms of asshole level. The individual on top of the list had to go.

The Hendrix Strat guy. Bill liked the idea. Burner phones, library computers, and silly disguises made it all happen. We paid cash for a similar guitar at Guitar Center, listed it on Craigslist, and set up the appointment to meet. While Bill walked towards him with a guitar case I clocked the bastard in the back of the head with a baseball bat. We laughed, put the corpse in the back of Bill's mom's 1997 Buick LeSabre, and headed to the desert to dump a body down an abandoned mine shaft. We threw a box of skyscraper demolition explosives down the shaft, activated the extraordinarily long fuse, and drove away victorious.

"Fuck that guy," Bill said.

Since weed people are lame people and they all live in a stupid weed world, Bill was having a problem with one of the dispensary owners—there's never just one owner of a dispensary—so Bill sold him an exploding electric bicycle.

Since we live in a stupid world, every neighborhood has one of those nosy neighbor types who's way too interested in everything everybody else is doing. I sure did. Someone like that sad fucker called the city and told them about my illegal gas-fueled fire pit—I had to assume it was him. I left an electric leaf blower on top of my trash can one day knowing he would take it. When all the lights flickered in my house thirty minutes later I knew he'd been electrocuted. Fried to a crisp.

Bill didn't like Dave's neighbor's dog, we don't kill dogs. For a while, we were putting at least one asshole out of their misery a week. Eventually, we ran out of real people we wanted to murder and channeled that energy into needlepoint and first-person shooter games.

THIRTY-FOUR

TROPICAL CRASH & BASH

UPS & DOWNS

WHEN IN DOUBT I CALL TAZ. "When did everything get to be so goddamn boring, Taz?"

"Jump on a plane, mate. You need a break. It's summer here and the weather is fantastic. Plenty of places you can stay as long as you like in Melbourne, Nagambie, Fremantle, all over. I just hired a Colombian, you can have Johanna for two days. Take her to the beach, teach her how to play the trombone, like Miles Davis."

"Don't you have a human resources department that can handle the second interviews?"

"Her sister turns 18 in three weeks. Call me when you land."

In the Qantas lounge at LAX, I devoured a lamb shank, some Vegemite, at least 18 ounces of mezcal, and two of the large

Xanax bars. The next thing I remember an attractive young man was removing his foam-covered lips from mine as a flight attendant's deft below-the-belt defibrillator deployment shocked me into consciousness. An ambulance met me on the tarmac and dropped me off at a bar in an alley when they couldn't stand my jokes anymore.

"Where the hell are you?" Taz asked.

"Australia. Whitehart Bar."

"Jesus. How the hell did you find that place?"

"Paramedics told me it was a hospital."

"I'll see you in ninety seconds."

"Was that you on TV?" Taz asked, ninety seconds later.

"No. I told them my name was Chip Conrad."

Taz said, "Let's go. You need sleep," as we walked down one sketchy alley and up another where he unlocked a stately door.

"People live here?" I asked.

"Just me. It's all offices and other bullshit around here."

The Taz building on narrow Niagara Lane was a brick warehouse building with a giant garage and office on the ground level, two floors of living space above that, then a tremendous roof deck.

"This place is unbelievable, Taz."

"I have loads of these. It only takes two prostitutes to cover the monthly expenses here. I have over a hundred at all times."

"Your company Christmas party must be the best," I said, in all sincerity.

"Many attendees call me the day after and tell me it sucked."

"You're right, I need sleep."

"I'll be back Monday, a dingo broke through the fence and ate a baby on my property in Queensland."

"I have a better idea than a fence for you people who seem to be the only people on Earth with a dingo problem," I said.

"Let me get a pen, I'll take notes," Taz said.

"Get some of those Ukrainian drones and make murdering dingos a video game. Kids can kill dingos from homes all over the world, all day, every day. Make it a contest. Like the Special Olympics."

"I might suggest that to the Governor. The fence builders won't like it, that's our second biggest industry."

"What's number one?"

"Ask Johanna. Make sure you tip her generously. And take her to some really nice places, she just landed this morning."

A day or so of sleep and a shower cleansed America from my pores, Johanna's arrival helped rejuvenate Black Patrick in many ways. She never learned my name is not Papi, but we shared ramen, coconut water, and awkward moments that I'll remember for a lifetime. Thank you, Johanna, wherever you are. Thank you.

"I see you found the hooks in the ceiling," Taz said when he joined me for a breakfast of champions in the kitchen of his Niagara Lane den of awesomeness.

"I like the Velcro wall."

"We're off to Nagambie, it's a special night at the speedway tonight."

The sign outside the speedway did, indeed, portend a special evening:

Tropical Fuck Storm & Nagambie Vineyards present
Ladies Crash & Bash Truck Doctor 69 Lapper!

Over the roar of old, smoke-belching junk cars, Gareth told me, "We're pressing an acoustic record, mate, it comes out in two weeks. Then we travel the roads of Australia for three weeks performing in the smallest towns we can find."

"Beautiful."

"Wait, there's more," infomercial guy Gareth said. "We have a heavy stoner rock psychedelic record ready. We want you to take the tapes back to L.A. and master it right now."

"Tapes?"

"Then we go on tour all over the world again."

"Let's do it!"

"Play our new shit for Dave, will ya? I think he'll like it."

Dave was waiting in the control room at Honker Studios when I arrived from the airport. His blank expression and serious demeanor were all business. *This had better be good.* I fired up the quarter-inch tape machine and we listened to the entire record from start to finish without a word spoken.

"Patrick, grab the tape and get in the car, we're going to see Howie." Ten minutes later we were in mastering engineer Howie's craftsman-style home in Highland Park staring in the face of gold and platinum records celebrating Howie's work. We climbed the stairs to Howie's attic studio and listened to the entire record from start to finish while Howie made tiny adjustments that turned amazing into phenomenal.

"Come back tomorrow morning," Howie told us. "This shit's epic. Epic."

Dave drove us back toward his place in silence. On the shortcut through South Pasadena he pulled over to the side of the road, turned off the engine, and told me, "Patrick, I want to take Tropical Fuck Storm on the road with my band of Daves. We've shipped over 100,000 records, CDs, and cassettes of the new record in three weeks."

"Let's call 'em right now and you can tell 'em. You and Howie are the only people outside of Australia who've heard that record."

"Where the fuck've you been, you tosser?" Gareth said as he answered the phone.

"Listen, young man, that's no way to address Diamond Dave," Dave said.

"Fuck you and your bullshit, Patrick. What do ya want?"

"You're doing three weeks in Mexico, a month or so in America, then Europe, Japan, and that giant kangaroo zoo where people like you live."

"I know, we told Patrick to make that happen. He never disappoints anyone but the ladies."

"Adios, Australia, work on your español!"

"We need Chip," Dave said. "I have a score to settle."

Professor Chip arrived to an honor guard of brass and woodwinds as a stunning woman in body paint and clown makeup directed Dave's exalted guests into his world. Chip's entourage of academic types were unprepared for the greatest night of their lives.

From his elevated perch overlooking the barbecue situation, Dave commanded the honor guard, "Señors, block the gates." A blast of horns signaled in the affirmative.

"Welcome, friends from near and far. Proceed immediately to the bar for the customary Flaming Dr. Pepper ceremony."

And, with that, the academics became wild and crazy party animals. Dave grabbed Chip and me and brought us into the house for a kitchen table conference.

"Gentlemen, I have a problem with a rival in the world of business I need your help to vanquish."

Chip asked, "Sammy?"

Dave just glared at Chip. "Sammy partnered with that white trash TV food guy to launch another tequila brand."

"Guy Ferrari. That shit's terrible," I said.

"I need a partner in the tequila business," Dave said. "What say you?"

"Tropical Fuck Storm," Chip said. "Dave's Tropical Tequila Storm. What's next, Dave?"

"Let's call Howie and see if he's done."

Around midnight Howie sent us an electronic copy of the new Tropical Fuck Storm record *Blasted* at which time Dave demanded silence and dropped the proverbial needle. We sent the master to the band in Australia. We didn't hear back but they posted a video clip of everyone running around a campfire and jumping in a lake. Everybody looked happy.

Chip turned the tequila business into a class project for one of his entrepreneur courses. Every class meeting started with a question: "Who is the enemy?"

"Sammy is the enemy! Fuck Sammy!" Something about hearing a classroom of merciless, cutthroat, and motivated business people say that in unison warmed Dave's heart.

"Dave, how can you afford to pay all these people? 20 band members, lights, sound—"

"I haven't spent a penny."

"What?"

"I've already sold the tequila distribution rights twenty times," Dave said.

"How?"

"We wrote the contracts right. One company buys the rights, when another company wants to pay them more for it, we have right of first refusal. We buy it back and sell it for more. We've done that twice in North America, Japan, and Asia, Three times in the U.K., Europe, and South America, and four times in Oceania. We haven't sold a drop of tequila and we've banked nine figures."

"You're using tequila money. That's brilliant, Dave."

"Wait until you see how the Brits are marketing the tequila in London, Scotland, and Ireland."

"Tropical Fuck Storm hasn't spent a penny on the road, ever."

"I know. The tequila biz covers all their touring expenses, you guys have grossed $20 million so far."

"We have?"

"Call your accountant."

"Chris, how much money do I have?"

"Let me run the numbers real quick—$8.64 million."

"Bill?"

"$12.772 million."

"Tropical Fuck Storm?"

"$9.4 million each. I don't know how you guys see some much revenue with almost zero expenses. You need more expenses."

"What do we spend it on?"

"Merchandise—buy a truckload. Marketing—do something stupid that generates a lot of press. Legal expenses —get arrested. Office supplies—"

"Got it. Does Bill know he's rich?"

"Oh yeah, he calls me almost every day. He's raking it in. Blackwater got a new CFO and he started paying Bill for window washing and shit like that again. The funniest one is landscaping."

"Can we expense strippers and hookers?"

"Yeah, take clients to whorehouses, get receipts, make sure you write their names on the receipts. It's categorized as an entertainment expense."

"If we hang a poster in the whorehouse is that an advertising expense?"

"Yes."

Since I knew I didn't need to work very hard the rest of my life, ten days into the American tour I went home and worked on setting up the triumphant end-of-tour shows in Los Angeles. The first thing I did was steal a motivated dude named Pedro Grant from that evil AEG cult and I sent him to join the Dave/Tropical Fuck Storm circus as road manager.

THIRTY-FIVE
FROM DOWN UNDER
LOS ANGELES

E VIL BASTARD TAZ CALLED ONE DAY, "One of my very most impressive salesladies from Melbourne wants to visit Los Angeles. I just sent a pic. She will be staying with you. Be your usual, charming self."

"I think you have the wrong number."

"Figure it out. Belle arrives Friday at 10:40 a.m., Qantas, LAX, you're welcome."

"Thanks, Taz, I think."

"By the way, The Tropical Fuck Storm pop-up store here in Melbourne is crackers. I'm opening in Sydney, Brisbane, Perth, and Nagambie Speedway. Ticket sales are tremendous. We're talking about adding additional shows in Melbourne and something really special at the speedway."

"Can we do an outdoor show at the Sydney Opera House like Thin Lizzy did in 1978?"

"That's a great idea! Epic!"

"Tropical Fuck Storm needs to open with 'Jailbreak' like Thin Lizzy did."

"I can see the whole thing in my mind clear as day, Patrick. We're doing it."

I forgot to ask Taz how long Belle was planning to stay, so I would invoke the as-if attitude and act as if she'd never be leaving or leaving the next day, based upon her initial response to my boorish behavior.

"Tell me all about Belle," I asked of my international visitor as she settled into the back seat of the Uber with me and posed for a selfie.

"I am an influencer," Belle said.

"Amazing, I am a bad influencer, we will get along just fine. What would you like to see and do while you're here in Los Angeles?"

"Show me your world. I want an authentic experience. Thank you, for hosting me, Patrick. Taz says you're top-notch."

"How long are you here, Belle?"

"I hope to see the Tropical Fuck Storm concert, they are Mum's favorites."

The wonderful woman named Belle and I roamed around the Los Angeles area exploring while I worked on logistics and promotion for the upcoming Tropical Fuck Storm shows. Belle became the world's biggest fan of Dave y los Tornados de Fuego, generating a fanbase for the band in Australia amongst her followers that quickly grew.

Astute businessman Dave called from the road one day and suggested Belle and I host a Japanese influencer. That's when I learned Belle was attached to me. She was all for it, so Yuki arrived from Tokyo to make us a throuple. Yuki's genuine enthusiasm for David Lee Roth y los Daves matched Belle's and they started dressing like the band members, posting clips and photos that created a fashion craze in Japan. Things were getting weird, that's the way it should be.

Alas, our time with Yuki was brief, she and Billthy Animal fell in love with each other at first sight. And then the same thing happened with Yuki and Ivy. The three of them put plans in motion to open a store called IVYUKI/Honker in Japan, we found out later.

With Yuki gone, mostly, Belle said, "We need a puppy," out of the blue one day.

"Why don't get another Asian woman, maybe Korean or Vietnamese, this time?" To Belle's credit, she explored all avenues and determined the adorable little dingo puppy was the best fit. The little guy we named Champ took over our world and became the boss.

THIRTY-SIX

CONQUERING HEROES

LOS ANGELES | JAPAN | AUSTRALIA

A S IS HIS CUSTOM, Dave returned to the Pasadena compound a conquering hero. The vintage and gleaming Dave y los Tornados de Fuego bus arrived at Dave's home the same way it had in every city and more than a few Waffle Houses across America for the past six weeks—with a lights-and-sirens police escort to announce arrival. A Japanese-themed fiesta raged within the compound's walls to greet the returning warriors. Dave leaped out of his shiny motor coach first, resplendent in his full glory as a band leader, followed by the rest of the Daves and Tropical Fuck Storm. Bill's samurai chonmage, kimono, hakama, and hige greatly impressed Dave and amused the Mexican and

Australian musicians. Belle and Yuki were in tears for various reasons.

Dave surveyed the scene within the compound as Bill handed him his trusty megaphone. Dave announced, "Ladies and gentlemen, by the power invested in me by the mystical and powerful chupacabras of Jalisco, I declare, the party starts now." No joke. The party went nuclear.

Carlito was excited to be home and even more excited about his acquisition of an essential guitar foot pedal on the road. "Dude, I found a vintage MXR Phase 90 at a pawn shop in Mobile, Alabama."

"Earl's?"

"Yes!"

"I know Earl. Does he still have that B.C. Rich Double Neck?"

"Yes! He has two. I almost bought one, those things are sick. I can't stop using the Phase 90."

"Don't. What's the highlight of the tour, so far?"

"The music, man. Our shit is really good. We keep getting heavier and heavier. All we listen to on the bus is Black Sabbath."

"Tune the whole band down a half-step, like Motörhead," I suggested.

"That's a great idea. Dave's vocals would sound meaner, too. Darker. All of the Daves want to play heavier, harder, darker music."

"You need more Marshalls. I don't think anybody's incorporating heavy, doom metal-type shit into your kind of music right now," I told Carlito, coming from a place of zero knowledge of this kind of music.

"You're right, nobody ever thinks about ways to move the music forward. People will be blown away or we'll all be blown away by the cartels."

Taz landed in town the next day and Dave, Taz, and myself met to nail down details of the Los Angeles, Japan, and Australia shows, and the associated activities.

Based on what Carlito told me about Dave y los Tornados de Fuego's evolution in a heavier direction, I proposed we record a live album in Los Angeles.

Carlito Bandido with more Marshalls. Back in the day when Carlito appeared regularly on The Oprah Winfrey Show and raved about Black Patrick books.

"Patrick," Dave responded, "do you know why we never released a live Van Halen record at the peak of our fame?"

"Yeah, because all of the live albums were fake and it was a lot more fun to record new material than go back and fix everything needed to save your live recordings."

"Good answer," Dave said. "I approve."

Some proposed having special guest stars join the bands onstage in Los Angeles as if they were the Foo Fighters or some shit like that. I was firmly against all of that horseshit, Lemmy was dead, what's the point? We debated that, and, in the end, I torpedoed every attempt to allow any other motherfuckers on the sacred ground of the TFS/Dave stage. Too fucking corny.

Bill, Ivy, and Yuki proposed Honker/IV7XI popup stores at the shows in Los Angeles, Melbourne, and Tokyo, which was approved. We all wondered if we should change the name of IV7XI or exploit 7XI's donkey-fucking career, that topic remained unresolved.

Taz proposed we turn the shows in Australia with Tropical Fuck Storm headlining into a traveling festival of 15 shows all over Australia, Tasmania, and New Zealand. Dave agreed to do the entire tour, Taz told him he'd anticipated that and booked venues. Ticket sales were brisk.

Dave asked about touring China, but somebody pulled a fire alarm, meeting adjourned.

THIRTY-SEVEN

WALKIN' THE DOG

CHANEL

B ELLE REMAINED IN HER HOMELAND WHEN THE AUSTRALIAN LEG OF THE TOUR ENDED. I went home to unwind in Los Angeles with my buddy Champ. Champ was overexcited upon my arrival and then supremely depressed when he realized his favorite person, Belle, did not return.

"Nothing lasts forever, Champ," I told the adolescent puppy bastard staring at me from his doggy bed with sad puppy dog eyes. "Nothing lasts forever."

Both Champ and I chose to forestall depression by taking to the streets of Los Angeles with gusto. Our adventures together brought us back to life as babe magnet Champ discovered women other than Belle and, importantly, variety and its positive ability to spice up life. One day, after visiting Bill in Pasadena, Champ and I met a stunningly gorgeous, yet incredibly stupid, woman and her puppy, Lulu, on the path through the arroyo. Lulu fell head-over-heels in love with Champ, Champ and I both wanted Lulu's mom more than anything, for different reasons, I hope.

The tallest and most beautiful woman in the world, Chanel, thinking about all of the things she wants to do to Black Patrick. Get in line, Chanel, get in line.

Lulu's mom, Chanel, and I became fast friends, meeting daily in the arroyo to walk our dogs. Lulu wanted Champ to be her boyfriend, but Champ didn't even see Lulu, which made Lulu want Champ even more. Chanel brought along other hot dog moms (hot dog moms?) sometimes. One day we stopped at Dave's house for a bottle of tequila and one thing led to another with Chanel on the beach. It was weird with doggies running around the outside of the tennis court's fence cheering us on, but Chanel's ability to focus is what made me fall in love with her.

And then things got complicated. Chanel revealed she belonged to a cult and was married to a man named Courtland. Anybody named Courtland—I'm talking first name here—deserves to die. More on that later. Chanel told me her cult was called MAGA and, if she tried to leave, an army of diaper-wearing lunatics in red hats would hunt her down and tell people wearing suits and holding microphones, "I always knew she was evil."

"Why don't you change your name?" I suggested.

Chanel told me, "Everybody in my family does that, it never seems to work."

"Let's kill your husband and move to Australia, right now."

"Thank you! I love you, Patrick."

Before Courtland's severed head finished rolling down the riverbed, Chanel expressed her appreciation in ways the first-class partitions of our overnight flight to Melbourne on a Qantas A-380 did not entirely shield from other passengers' view.

Bill called and asked, "Why is Champ here with a weird little Pomeranian?"

"Because we didn't want my girlfriend's husband to end up like NDGT."

"Copy."

It didn't take me long to figure out I needed to keep Chanel busy all the time. The cult she belonged to brainwashed her and a lot of others in my intellectually-lacking homeland to believe some crazy shit. One evening at dinner with Taz and one of his concubines, Chanel said, "I hear the Chinese are draining the oceans next week."

A prolonged period of silence ended only when Taz finished an impressive assortment of facial contortions and asked Chanel, "Draining the oceans?"

Chanel explained, "The Chinese navy is draining the oceans and planting flags all over the ocean floor to claim new Chinese territory all over the world. They already own Greenland."

"That makes sense," I said, in an attempt to stop the bleeding.

The stunned and barely coherent Taz asked Chanel, "Where does the water go?"

"It drains."

Taz drove us all back to the Niagara Lane hideout, sent the ladies upstairs to make sandwiches, and then summoned me to the office. As he powered up the white noise generator he asked me, "Are you fucking stupid?"

"I know I'm not as smart as I was before I met Chanel. Why?"

"She's dumb as a drunk dingo cunt and not even close to an Aussie six."

"In America Chanel is a solid seven and considered by many a stable genius."

"We need to get rid of her, stupid people are dangerous," Taz said.

"I agree. Do dingos eat dingbats?"

"Send her back," Taz said.

"Chanel is always telling me how much she misses her mee-maw in Korea."

"Perfect. I know a guy who can put her on a plane to North Korea right now."

"That was easy."

Chanel went to South Korea to visit her grandmother and was never seen again.

THIRTY-EIGHT

THE WOLF HOWLS

PASADENA

B ILL FOUND SOME HASHISH IN THE MAIL AT DAVE'S HOUSE, so he was on another planet when I showed up at the tennis court beach after walking Dr. Drew's dogs.

"I know the *W* in sword is silent, but I'm confused about the *L* in wolf," Bill bravely admitted.

"You think it's pronounced woof?"

"I don't, to me it sounds like onomatopoeia when you say wolf that way. My friend says Howlin' Woof."

"Here's how we solve that problem, Bill. We howl like a big wolf for the Howlin' part, then we woof like a baby wolf for the Wolf part. New rule. Try it."

Bill did and birds fell out of the sky again.

What the fuck?

"What was that?" I asked Bill.

"The neighbor."

I practiced saying Howlin' Wolf a couple of times then asked Bill, "Bill, how long are you gonna live at Dave's place? You should buy a house. You must have enough money."

"Fuck that. I never want to own a house. There hasn't been a single day since I got here where something isn't broken or blowing up. *Ka-boom!*"

"Buy a condo, then you don't have to worry about most of that shit."

"Are you crazy? I don't pay rent here. Don't jinx it."

"Buy something. This won't last forever. How much money do you have saved?"

"I have no idea. I don't want to know. As long as the ATM card works and the credit card works I don't need shit."

"It's not a bad idea to call Chris and ask him."

"It's a terrible idea. I've never even talked to the guy. He sends me shit, I sign it, that's all, folks."

"Have you been to his office? If he's stealing our money he's not spending it on lavish office decor."

"No gold toilet?"

"No toilet, period. Everybody in the office has to walk down the street to 7-11 and beg the cashier/owner to use his filthy restroom. The guy makes 'em explain why, then he says, 'One time only! You buy something!' Chris is often observed strolling down Hawthorne Boulevard taking a bite out of one of those 7-11 hot dog things and throwing the rest of it into traffic. If you're driving southbound on Hawthorne, you can see a pile—"

"We should buy Chris a gift card for the port-a-potty company for Christmas," Bill suggested.

"He's probably their accountant, he'd just refund it and take the cash."

"I don't want to know how much money I have. If it's $5 or 5 million dollars I'll freak out just the same."

The evil Black Patrick was losing patience fast and had one of those momentary freak-outs when he thought he'd lost his drugs, again. "Bill, I know how much money you have. And I know you know how rich you are. Nobody cares if you have a dollar or a billion dollars. Where are you gonna go if Dave tells you to leave?"

"Well, Neil deGrasse Tyson was my plan B…"

"Did the cops in Mexico ever find Neil deGrasse Tyson's stolen head?" I asked.

"Who cares? Dave wrote a song about creepy dead neighbor Neil DGT. It's great. I don't even like that kind of music. It's called, 'Tráeme la Cabeza de Neil deGrasse Tyson,' I think."

"Neil died doing what he loved doing most," I said.

"Giving head to dogs?"

"I never said that."

"Maybe I can move in with Wolfgang," Bill proposed.

"What I want to know about Wolfgang is, why is that guy so fat? And still not nearly as heavy as your girlfriend? Didn't Wolfgang's mom do commercials for Weight Watchers or some shit like that?"

"Dave says Wolfie won't play a show in a town without a Cheesecake Factory."

"That's smart, it's a good thing there aren't any towns without a Cheesecake Factory in the United States."

"When Wolfgang was on tour with the band they had to bring their own solid steel tables for craft services. The commonly-provided folding tables backstage kept collapsing, injuring people, and venues were getting killed by the workers' compensation claims."

"Watch out, 7XL and Wolfgang have a lot in common."

"One guy lost a leg. Buried under 40 pounds of pasta, a mountain of some kind of bullshit egg rolls—"

"Those Cheeseburger Spring Rolls are unreal," I interjected.

"Totally. Wolfgang walked around smelling like those fucking things 24/7. The poor craft services guy was buried under the pasta—"

"What was the pasta?"

"The pasta rotated depending on the day of the week. That show, it was one of the shrimp pastas that smell up the whole arena."

"That shit is fucking awful."

"So, the pasta, the spring rolls, a mountain of meat loaves larger than two Meat Loafs, at least a dozen grilled rib eyes, a heaping pile of flatbreads—"

"Did the cheesecake survive?"

"Believe it or not, they always ordered one of each, so there were more than 30 cakes every night. A heroic effort was made, sadly, cheesecake number eleven, I think it was the Chocolate Caramelicious, was lost, along with a leg. The band dedicated the encore that night to Jeremy."

"Somebody Get me a Doctor?"

"Poundcake."

"That's a Van Hagar song."

"Wolfgang sang it. Tears streaming down his face, obviously starving."

"I don't like fat people, but I don't wanna see the guy starve."

"Dave said Wolfgang's tour bus kept rolling over until they added a shitload more suspension. That worked most of the time, but, ultimately, engineers from the locomotive division of Caterpillar had to be called in to install massive gyroscopes to keep the bus level."

"So, everything's okay now?"

"Well, not exactly. Wolfgang lost some refrigerator space. There wasn't a whole lot to begin with, either. The bathroom, the doorways, the seats, everything is massive."

"I'm no expert, however, if the great American freight rail system cannot provide Wolfgang with the services he requires, Wolfgang might want to invest in a used C-130."

"They looked at a C-17 in New Zealand. Alex couldn't stop laughing, so that didn't work."

"Do you think we are such a blessed country because we have Cheesecake Factory, or, we're such an amazing country we created Cheesecake Factory?"

Keep it down over there!

"Who the fuck was that?"

"The nosy cunt neighbor, again, he listens to everything going on here. He needs to get a life."

"And, after that, we make him die. WWBAD?"

"What?"

"What would Billthy Animal do?"

"The hammer's gonna make him die."

THIRTY-NINE

DEEP DARK DIRTY LITTLE SECRET

INNER SPACE

I DIDN'T CARE ANYMORE. In fact, I woke up every morning and said the same thing: "I don't care anymore. I don't care anymore. I don't fucking care anymore."

The freedom one feels when not caring anymore is unmatched by any feeling except the feeling of not fucking caring anymore. The fucking means everything. All the time. Everything. All the time.

Life can take its toll when you're living rock 'n' roll. Up all night, sleep all day, nothing good on TV, anyway. Even if you eat right and smoke dynamite, shit happens.

Maybe it was all of the women. Maybe it was all of the drugs. Maybe it was all of the travel. Maybe drinking tequila and laughing is detrimental to a human's health. I didn't know and there was no reason to stop and try to figure that out.

Black Patrick—hammered, confused, suicidal, on drugs, and hallucinating.

Everybody knew more than me. Everybody was smarter than me. Everybody was better than me at everything. The reason suburban hellholes are suburban hellholes is only because of the people who never seem to shut the fuck up, yet never say anything worth listening to, never do a goddamned thing, and can't stop telling you all about what you're doing and how it's not good enough.

As a younger man, I knew how to cure this disease we now know as depression: leave Orange County forever. This might not work for you, however, a good rule of thumb is to leave any metropolitan area or state with fewer than 5 million people. And eliminate every part of America as your destination save for Los Angeles, New York, Chicago, and Boston. Maybe include New Orleans. The rest of America is a toilet.

Ideally, you will be one of the few, the proud Americans who use a passport. Then you can escape to a more civilized society such as those found in Scandinavia and Spain, for example. Canada, Japan, and Australia are fine choices, too. It doesn't matter where you move, as long as you move.

Here's the dirty little secret about this book: it's all propaganda. Every word is carefully calculated and chosen based on its ability to prompt the people of the United States of America and the rest of the world to listen to more rock 'n' roll at a higher volume more often. The end, what a great story. Thanks for cheering me up.

PART 5
THERE GOES TOKYO

FORTY
COME TASTE JAPAN
PASADENA

B ILL LED ME DOWN TO THE SECRET BUNKER under Dave's tennis court beach to a dark, spooky room with a conference table set up in a manner not unlike a presidential cabinet meeting. Tent cards with names, etc.

"Check this out," Bill said as he used an iPad to start a presentation.

"What the fuck?" I exclaimed. "What the hell is that?"

"It's Honker Records Japan."

"That building looks familiar."

"It's Tower Records in Shibuya. At least it used to be Tower Records. Yuki's dad owns the company that owned the building. Taz bought it."

While I was dealing with world wars inside my head on sabbatical, the motherfuckers had been busy.

Dave arrived on fire and in successful businessman mode. "Ladies and gentlemen, how do? Thank you kindly for sharing some time with us, my name is David Lee Roth and I wholeheartedly support this message and I can't wait to see everybody in Shibuya real soon. Bill asked me to MC today's event, so let me introduce us all to each other."

The phone gang included Akira-san, Yuki, CPA Chris, Taz, Tropical Fuck Storm, and Chip Conrad. Carlito Bandito, Ivy, Bill, Dave, and I were all together in the Pasadena bunker.

Dave brought us all up to speed. "Taz bought the building from Akira-san, both are equity partners in Honker Japan. Bill will run three floors of Honker Records, Yuki and Ivy will manage three floors of IVYUKI. Carlito Bandito is the brains behind a full floor of Carlito Bandito Guitars, Yours truly shall endeavor to parch thirsts and fill stomachs with Dave's Cafe on the ground floor and, to top it all off, be of service at Dave's Tropical Tequila Storm on the top floor.

"We purchased all of the fixtures, equipment, supplies, and inventory from Tower Records and retained every employee who wished to work with us—all of them. We elevated the pay of every employee, added certain, amazing benefits to their compensation packages, and we will present every member of our Japanese family with a special welcome gift at our grand opening fiesta exactly 73 days from today.

"Bill and Ivy have scoured the countryside of the United States of America acquiring spectacular merchandise—we have eight containers en route as we speak. Yuki is doing the same in Japan. Carlito has procured an extraordinary collection of guitars and amplifiers for the guitar store to complement the generous donations from his exclusive Japanese partner, Ibanez. Honker merchandise is predicted to be remarkably popular in Japan, therefore we are manufacturing 124,000 units of high-quality, American-made apparel as we speak."

Taz. On fire. Sexy.

"Bill, Carlito, Ivy, and myself will be in Tokyo next week to finalize architectural details. Bill, Ivy, and Carlito will remain in Tokyo to work with contractors, meet with local vendors, and get a general sense of the scene and industry. Black Patrick, when you're ready, get over there.

"The formidable juggernaut known as Chip Conrad has assembled a class of five Japanese-speaking international business students selected to accompany him to Tokyo to live, learn, and work alongside us. Several more Japanese students will join his party in Tokyo.

"Taz has negotiated an incredible, unbelievable, unheard-of package of marketing and advertising with our tequila distributor
in Japan. He'll bring the greatest band in the fucking world, Tropical Fuck Storm, to Tokyo for two weeks to make friends, promote Honker Records, and perform on the Honker Stage a couple of times.

"Carlito Bandito is off to Tokyo in a couple of days on the flying Bandito to meet with his Japanese team, by the way.

"CPA Chris will travel to Tokyo with two of his Japanese-speaking accountants early next month.

"I will be in and out of Tokyo endlessly and ritually. Our North American tequila distributor will pay to send all 20 of the Daves to Japan for two weeks. Nobody in that town will be able to turn around, ride a subway, or eat sashimi without seeing one or more of the Daves.

"And, finally, it is with deep humility, I know I speak for everybody on the team, we all look forward to joining Akira-san and Yuki at the Yamaha home for a barbecue in 6 weeks."

Dave was on fire, rallying an all-star team to kick some ass.

"The Japanese operation is Honker Records Japan, inc. The name of the store is Honker Records. The following appointments have been agreed upon unanimously and enthusiastically:

Honker Records Japan, inc.

  Chairman: Akira-san
  CEO: Taz
  COO: Yuki
  CFO: CPA Chris

"All assembled here are hereby appointed Board Members of Honker Japan, excluding Tropical Fuck Storm. After a moment of silence, please join me as we shout the Honker Japan credo.

"Fuck Sammy!"

After the call wrapped up, Dave looked Carlito dead in the eye and said, "Carlito, parlay your momentary fame as a guitar player into a great place to land when nobody gives a shit about your music anymore, which could be any minute."

"Bill, whatever inventory you have acquired will be gone the weekend the store opens. Buy more record stores."

"Ivy, you are a beautiful and intelligent woman. Don't forget us when you're the Queen. For now, send more merchandise to Japan."

"Patrick, you are about to be more wealthy than all of us combined. Go to Tokyo right now, talk to a couple of reporters in your customarily humble way. Task Chip's team with sourcing licensing deals for Honker. You're going to go nuclear with that shit in Japan overnight. Two words: Cash. In. You're not looking at millions, it's billions, motherfucker"

"I thought I was just meeting Bill for coffee. When were you guys gonna tell me about this?"

"We almost didn't," Dave said.

"Is Yuki's name Yuki Yamaha?" I asked.

"You didn't know?"

"Know what?"

"Fuck. Her dad runs Yamaha Musical Instruments. How the fuck do you fuckers stumble into this shit over and over again?"

Bill said, "We're on a mission from God."

After the meeting wrapped up Bill, Carlito, and I hit the beach and concentrated heavily on alcohol intake.

"Carlito, are you famous somewhere?" I asked.

Bill interjected, "*Mean Chords* is the best-selling instrumental guitar album in history."

Carlito said, "I'm like a Kardashian in Japan. The reality TV show crew gets here in half an hour."

"I'm living in Dave's condo in Tokyo," Bill said. "It's a penthouse with a pool on top of a building filled with karaoke bars, restaurants, hostess bars, batting cages, miniature golf, a bowling alley…"

Carlito asked me, "Wanna go hit a few guitar stores?"

We jumped in Carlito's rented box truck and hit the road. When I asked Carlito why he was driving a box truck he said, "You'll see."

Carlito's blistering pace and impressive navigational skills saw us buy guitars at six retail stores, a recording studio going out of business, and a couple of guitar collectors' homes in about nine hours. The box truck was fully loaded with an obscene amount of Ibanez gear Carlito bartered for the mostly vintage American guitars and amps we acquired. Brand-new Ibanez guitars were not in great demand at the time, so Carlito ended the day with 42 items suitable for the Japan store.

"I find myself hating ZZ Top and Cheap Trick more and more every day," Carlito said. "Billy Gibbons and Rick Nielsen own all of the guitars, man. That's stupid."

"No shit. How can these guitar companies keep cranking out thousands of guitars every day and there's no cool shit in the stores?"

"Keeping that store stocked is going to be impossible, man."

"I have an idea, Carlito. Let's call Chip. Every college kid in America, and twenty other countries, thinks he's the shit. Chip finds one guitar geek/student to act as your personal shopper. Ibanez sends the student 50 guitars, Chris sends him 20 grand, he or she hits the road shopping for guitars. It might work."

Sure enough, Chip found a guitar-playing student, Ibanez sent the student 50 guitars, Chris sent him $20,000, Carlito received 19 vintage guitars, a killer Marshall 100-watt head, and a few foot pedals two weeks later. Carlito told CPA Chris to wire the guy more cash and Ibanez to send him more guitars, Cliff in Boston became the Vice President of Purchasing for Carlito Bandito Guitars, International, almost overnight.

Bill and Ivy utilized the Carlito Bandito purchasing method with similar success—the world was at peace. During our guitar-hunting travels across California, Carlito told me, "Every single Dave has an endorsement deal. All of them. It's crazy. They all want to play multiple instruments so they can land more deals. Accordion Dave is also Cowbell Dave, Mouth Harp Dave, Washboard Dave—"

"Accordion Dave found a washboard company to endorse him? That guy's a fucking genius. Simply finding a washboard company is an accomplishment."

"That's nothing, Dave Van Trumpet found an air raid siren company," Carlito said.

I thought about Carlito's guitar store for a minute. Ibanez was promised half of the guitar store space and the rest would be used/vintage gear from America. "People are gonna want to buy other instruments but you're not selling anything but electric guitars and amps, right? Stock that other shit but don't keep it on the sales floor."

"How would that work?"

R.I.P. Tower Records. Again.

"Customer wants an accordion, tell them what you can get, you can order it, you'll have it in an hour. Collect payment, give the customer a coupon for free food at Dave's place. Grab the item from the back room, text the customer, boom. Make the instrument manufacturers send you everything on consignment so you never pay for it. Get a bunch of that shit up front. And buy as many guitars as you can right now. Everything you buy will sell and guitars only appreciate in value."

"Thanks, Billy Gibbons."

Back at the Pasadena complex, Dave said, "This might be a good time to call Chip about Honker licensing, P-dog," so I did.

"Chip, I need your help putting the Honker deals together. I'm told he's the next Hello Kitty in Japan."

"Ha, that's funny," Chip said. "The president of Sanrio is the father of one of my students. Your timing is perfect. That Sanrio company is on fire. We'll meet with those guys in Tokyo."

"Great, get it done, tell me what you want to be paid, onward!"

"Dude, you're not paying me a penny. Your goofy school idea turned me into an international celebrity and I'm even more filthy rich than I was before. Cash comes in from every direction. All I do is listen to people and give advice all day. You have no idea how grateful I am."

"Thanks, Chip, you're too kind. I'm going to the airport."

FORTY-ONE

NO HONKER NO LIFE

TOKYO DIDN'T KNOW WHAT HIT 'EM. Without warning, 20 identically dressed Mexican musicians landed in Japan's largest city and spread out all over town. Like everybody's hero, Dave, much of their travels were environmentally-conscious excursions via bicycle. At any given moment authorities confirmed as many as nine banda cells operating in Tokyo. Reports said the fashionably attired aliens demanded nothing but mezcal and cerveza, two items Japan's Earthy citizens were largely unfamiliar with. At least twice a day the entire population of small, shiny people wearing large hats and intricately embroidered formal wear converged perform the *Relationship of Command* album start-to-finish sans vocals, guitar, bass, and drums for Tokyo's unsuspecting masses.

The first thing I did when I landed in Japan was find a Shibuya punk rock atelier to produce a limited edition of 600 gold, satin-like, fringed, Honker mariachi jackets and 100 black leather versions. The apparel manufacturer told me, "I will have these for you in three weeks."

Taggers.

"Three weeks? Can we get them sooner?"
"No."
"No?"
"We do not live the Godfathers lifestyle in Japan."
"The pizza place or the movies?"

"The band. We do not do *Birth, School, Work, Death* like you stupid Americans. Go away, come back in three weeks, you cunt."

Anybody operating a business out of a 350-square-foot storefront with GBH and NOFX posters on the walls who calls a customer placing an order for $87,000 a cunt is someone I need, so I offered Aiko a job at Honker Japan on the spot. She said "Fuck you." I sent all of the Daves to her store the next day where Los Daves attracted a huge crowd resulting in massive sales at Aikoland. We did that every day for a week. The phenomenal Honker jackets landed in less than two weeks. We were all impressed, we ordered more.

I met with toy companies and ordered all kinds of goofy Honker action figures and silly tchotchkes. And I found confectioners to produce Honker suckers and other treats. Then I the vending machine mafia agreed to place Honker toys and candy in vending machines all over Japan.

Carlito introduced me to his posse at Ibanez and we allowed them to build every crazy Honker Guitar design we could think of, for a price. Nothing excited us more than the double-neck relic collection inspired by beat-up B.C. Rich guitars found in Alabama pawn shops. Every guitar was a relic, meaning it was intentionally damaged so it would look old and fucked-up. Dave's rooftop jacuzzi saw more ash than ass some days. Not much ebony, sadly. The occasional Brazilian. We all miss Mahogany.

Thanks to Japanese efficiency, Honker Records arrived and survived prepared for monumental success on time. As soon as the big party was over.

FORTY-TWO

THUNDER FORWARD AT LIGHTNING SPEED

TOKYO

T HE FRIGHTENINGLY GORGEOUS WOMAN in the luminescent electric green dress looked like a hot jalapeño pepper to me. A lady wearing anything cut on the bias is my kind of gal. Galapeño might have been the only person at the Honker Records Grand Opening Fiesta having more fun than me. Dancing, laughing, slamming flaming Dr. Peppers—I had to avert my gaze / stare and wipe. My brow, you sicko.

A strong, feminine voice spoke to me from behind, "I am told by the captain you are responsible for the unavoidable and hideous visuals we now enjoy all over Tokyo."

"Yes, and, not only the Mexicans in goofy outfits, the clown guy, too."

"Honker?"

"If you insist."

"You put Tower Records out of business for this clown nonsense?"

"Yes. I like to think I've put Tower Records out of business more than once. Let's begin again."

"Can you?"

"Patrick. Black Patrick. A pleasure to meet you. Thank you for being here, it means the world to Honker."

"Kiko, just Kiko. Kiko as in 'Kiko needs more tequila, por favor, mi amor.'"

Kiko was trouble, so I introduced her to all of my friends and most of Dave's horn section in hopes she would maneuver that target my heat-seeking missile was locked on to, armed, and ready to fire at, right up that exhaust nozzle of hers, away from my guidance system. Kiko charmed and impressed all who dared engage her loveliness, none more than me.

"Kiko, we are doomed."

"Climate change leading to the collapse of human civilization before 2030?"

"Worse."

"Kiko, who is this captain you speak of?"

"Kangaroo. The Australian man who offered me a job as a waitress at his winery in Nagambie. Nagambie? He wouldn't stop touching me. Old Australians are almost as creepy as old Americans."

"Okay, here's the plan. You walk up to Captain Kangaroo and ask him how many more babies have to be eaten by dingos before he fixes the fence around his 7-11. Then, whatever he babbles for an answer, you slap him in the face as hard as you can, say, 'I had to pay for my own abortion!' and then walk away. I'll scream, 'You bastard!' at Captain Kangaroo and follow you to the elevator. It's our only way out of here."

Kiko's performance stunned and amazed the crowd. David Lee Roth didn't stop laughing for at least 15 minutes, according to witnesses and surveillance camera footage. Bill was last seen howling with laughter face down on the floor kicking it and pounding on it. Kiko demonstrated incredible acting skills, phenomenal, however, to confirm her thespian abilities I applied the Bill Hicks test. Flying colors. Flying colors.

I offered Kiko a ride home, but she refused and said, "I'm not going home alone as long as you live, Daddy."

A lot to unpack there. And the opposite of that. Kiko's dream was to be an actress in Hollywood, we gathered a few things and went to the airport. As luck would have it, Qantas upgraded us to first class on the A-380 non-stop flight to Los Angeles. Never trust anyone who says history does not repeat itself.

Somewhere over the Aleutian Islands we both began to sober up and wondered what the hell was going on. That's when Black Patrick shifted into *as if* mode. "Kiko, if we want to be together there must be no hesitation, zero doubt, complete trust, and true love."

"And then what happens," Kiko asked, as if she were taking the final exam of an improv class.

"We thunder forward at lightning speed."

I've seen women laugh before, but this was a little different. Maybe the slight language barrier caused Kiko to believe my earnest request for thunder and lightning was in jest. All I know is Kiko's howls and screams drowned out the pilot's announcements and annoying infants on the plane. Why are people still having kids, anyway?

"Kiko, what are we going to do with the rest of our lives?" I asked the woman who I would be spending the rest of my life with.

"I will be an actress in Hollywood."

"I made a film last year."

"No, you did not."

"Yes, I did. Check my IMDB."

"Executive producer? I can't believe this?"

Thank you, Tropical Fuck Storm. "It's right there on the internet."

"I can't believe this. You're the only executive producer I've ever blown before I found out they were an executive producer."

"Do you hear that sound? That's the sound of Kiko hitting the jackpot."

The phone rang, Taz was on the other end of the line. I answered, "You bastard!" Kiko laughed.

"We have a big problem here. The store's open and Dave's still wearing the stupid curly wig and calling himself the Red Docker."

"What's a docker?"

"It's when a man shoves his penis in another man's little hole—"

"Oh, that."

"He insists on calling the cafe Sammy's Shit Shack and he's making the waitresses jump on trampolines. Where are you?"

"About to land in Los Angeles."

"Why did that woman slap me?"

"You'll never know, Captain Kangaroo."

"Call Chip later. He's at the hospital with Yuki's dad, but I think they got a great deal done for you and Honker."

"Taz, you need to come to Los Angeles. I need your help."

"Kiko, I'm not ready to be home and deal with real-world things, let's go to Las Vegas."

"No. I will take care of the real world for you. As long as you treat me like a princess."

"I've never noticed Kings treating princesses well."

"What are you the king of, King Patrick."

"The blues. I'm the last King standing. Albert—gone. B.B.—gone. Freddie—gone... Black Patrick King is all we have left."

"You're the king of the blues?"

"Yes, let's go see Champ. You're about to change Champ's world."

FORTY-THREE
KIKO CONQUERS AMERICA

PASADENA

"A M I GOING TO BE GETTING PHONE CALLS at all hours for the rest of my life?"

"Probably," Taz answered. "We have a real problem, now. Chris and Chip are concerned, they say it's an existential crisis."

"Existential crises never turn into real problems. Existential is a word stupid people use to scare other stupid people. What's going on?"

"Chip's crew analyzed all of their market research, Chris and company reviewed the findings and agreed. We're going to sell out of nearly all of our merchandise by the end of our second day open."

"What won't we sell out of?"

"XL, XXL, and XXXL Honker T-shirts. Japan isn't Orange County, there is no market for obesity-sized clothing."

"If the inventory's all wiped out, close the store and tell everyone we were unprepared and we'll reopen when we have new shit to sell. Unless you're afraid of all the free fucking, worldwide, fucking press."

"Yeah, we'll have people lined up outside the store around the block and halfway to China if we close and reopen."

"Bill and Dave okay?"

"Not really, all they have to do is look at each other and the clock starts on 45 minutes of screaming laughter."

"Sorry, Taz, I'm entirely responsible for the slap."

"Dave added the Abortion Burger to the menu at Sammy's House of Shit. Chris is out looking for a bigger safe. Is Kiko gone, yet?"

"Yes, she is effectively gone. That little fucker, Champ, stole her heart, those two are inseparable."

"Hi, Captain Kangaroo!" Kiko said.

"If things get worse at home I'm leaving. Kiko and Champ won't even notice I'm gone."

"It's your fault for connecting every living thing to other living things."

"Isn't that what we're on this fucking planet to do?"

"Yes, according to the employee code of conduct for the ladies in Melbourne, at least. Where did Kiko come from?"

"Hell!" Kiko screamed.

"Kiko was on a first date with some dude at the Mexican restaurant across the street, the guy was a douchebag, she looked out the window and saw Bill puking all over himself on the sidewalk, two of the Daves doing unspeakable sexual things with each other, and somebody walking into the building with a donkey. I presume Chip ordered the donkey, for some reason. Anyway, Kiko, in her infinite wisdom, recognized a legendary fiesta and crashed the party."

"True story!" Kiko said.

"You are a very lucky man. Patrick. Try not to fuck this one up, Kiko. Go buy a couple of record stores, please. We need product."

"Fuck that. If you see Dave let him know we're on our way over to his place to eat mushrooms and watch Champ fly across his tennis court beach."

Over at Dave's compound, the most amazing woman I had ever met asked, "Whose house is this?"

"My friend Dave owns it. You probably met him on the luckiest night of your life. Like me, he will never forget you."

"Why doesn't he have any furniture."

"He's evolved to a higher level of consciousness. We're listening to Tropical Fuck Storm at high volume until we run out of tequila."

"I love that band," Kiko said. "So many mean chords."

"Mean chords. Mean everything. You mean everything to me, Kiko."

Before things went all the way to sappy town I called Tokyo to check in with Carlito Bandito.

"If Chip and Chris are right, we're fucked. Totally fucked," Carlito said.

"How's Dave?"

"Which one?"

"Touché. Hang in there, Bandito. In times of uncertainty go outside and stare at Honker's miserable face on the outside of that building and realize it could all be much worse."

"Tokyo doesn't have a Cheesecake Factory."

"That's why I came home. Kiko's never been to Cheesecake Factory or Sizzler."

"I'm 99 percent sure Dave's serving donkey tacos. Mainly because the sign I'm looking at says 'Sammy's Donkey Tacos' in the restaurant."

"He should sell whale tacos."

"Winner, winner, dolphin dinner."

Kiko returned to Tennis Beach from the ladies' room and asked, "Is this David Lee Roth's house?"

"Yes, it sure is, beautiful."

"Van Halen is my grandfather's favorite band!"

Yikes. Grandfather? I'll get around to asking Kiko how old she is at some point.

"I like Dave's house," Kiko said.

"Do you want a house like this?"

"Yes."

"Okay, here's the plan. We barbecue, eat lunch, stop by Honker USA, then we buy a house."

"Do you want me to make sandwiches? That will be faster."

"You know how to make sandwiches?"

And that was the first time Kiko slapped me in a non-sexual situation.

The crew at IVRIP and Kiko fell in love with each other while Champ lost his mind smelling everything and everyone in the store. I went next door to see Robbo in Honker Records. Robbo reported, "I just sent two containers to Japan yesterday. I sent two last week and two the week before that. We charge Japan a $10,000 per container handling fee, so the record store doesn't even have to sell anything and it turns a profit."

"Who's downstairs?"

"Some reality show assholes. They're off this week. They brought some weird props, you should check it out."

I walked into Honker Studios. Since when is porn considered reality TV? When I opened the door to IVRIP Studios and heard someone playing Rachmaninoff's Second Piano Sonata on the Steinway, I crashed on the couch in the control room, closed my eyes, and listened to majestic music fill the subterranean adult film set. What a beautiful piece. When it was over, a beautiful piece named Kiko found me and said, "Hey, there's a sex swing in here!" And that's when I locked the door and turned on the RECORDING light.

Champ remained with his superfans at IVRIP while Kiko and I drove around Pasadena looking at houses for sale. We saw a couple of winners. I learned Kiko couldn't wait to have a home where her sisters could come visit, including her twin, Miko. That's when I became a motivated buyer. We visited a couple of record stores, and Kiko found items I had no idea Japanese people might be interested in. We bought everything decent at a couple of Guitar Centers, then we filled the rest of Dave's pimped-out serial killer van with used books destined for Shibuya. At In-N-Out Burger Kiko ordered a Double-Double and all of the In-N-Out Burger T-shirts they had in sizes smaller than large. That was the first time she said, "Trust me."

Upon return to IVRIP, a catatonic Champ occupied a dog bed with a commanding view of the sales floor on the landing of the stairs leading to the mezzanine. A sparkly sign reading *Champ!* surrounded by hearts and kisses hung above his sleepy head. Champ was exhausted from an afternoon of exhilaration. Kiko was slightly wounded by Champ's lack of enthusiasm for her. Join the club, Kiko.

Before we could get in any more trouble, Kiko, Champ and I returned home for a relaxing evening on the couch in front of a television. "Is this your job? Visiting places and talking to people?"

"Sometimes. What do you do?"

"I completed my undergraduate studies at the University of Tokyo, waiting one year to start the graduate program."

"What do you want to do next?"

"Environmental Sciences or Musicology. I will attend graduate school because there are no jobs available in Environmental Sciences or Musicology I want in Japan."

I almost said, "Let's start a company," but I promised myself I would stop doing that.

FORTY-FOUR

HEADING OUT TO THE HIGHWAY

AMERICA

K IKO WANTED TO SEE AMERICA, so we flew to the East Coast and endeavored to drive around until we couldn't stand it anymore. We landed in Boston, rented a big, environmentally irresponsible sport utility vehicle, and hit the road. Kiko selected the destinations, I told her I didn't want to know where we were going, we saw some strange things in stranger places I would have never visited without a demented Japanese woman navigating.

Once Kiko discovered the wonderful world of the American thrift store our travels morphed into a shopping spree. Between Boston and Chattanooga, we must have visited a hundred thrift stores, pawn shops, musical instrument stores, record stores, and bookstores. And then there were the flea markets, swap meets, garage sales, yard sales, and estate sales. Kiko insisted we buy every old banjo and beat-up acoustic guitar we saw, resulting in her second, "Trust me."

Things got weird in Kentucky when the guy at the shipping company we stopped at to send goods to Robbo asked, "Are y'all pickers?"

"Well—"

Before I could say *Fuck no!* shipping guy said, "My cousin has a barn full of banjos."

Kiko put banjo barn man's address in her navigation system and the second leg of our American tour began.

Kiko said, "We don't have such a thing in Japan."

"Why not?"

"World War II."

"Shit happens…"

Kiko and I wound our way from Tennessee, into Arkansas, back through Kentucky and West Virginia, then Ohio, Indiana, and Illinois before we declared victory and celebrated our tomb raiding of America in Chicago. The dog-sitting angels at IVRIP lifted our spirits immeasurably throughout our travels with clips and videos from their escapades with Champ, whose Instagram and TikTok made him a puppy influencer across the globe. We missed the little guy, so we headed home.

By the time we returned to Los Angeles the first containers of merchandise from our American treasure hunt hit the shelves in Tokyo to tremendous acclaim. The joke items we shipped to Shibuya designed to amuse, anger, and delight Bill, Dave, Ivy, and Carlito excited our Japanese customers the most proving, once again, none of us know shit.

Kiko went back to Japan to see the family, Champ and I were bummed, and, right about the same time, Bill and Dave returned to Pasadena.

"Kiko wants me to buy us a house like yours," I told Dave.

"Can you afford it," Dave asked.

"Yeah," I responded, "I just sold 25% of Honker to some sheik in Saudi Arabia who owns an oil company."

"We do this today, Black Patrick. Today. The neighbor behind me called me yesterday and said he wanted to sell his house to me. I told him, 'I want yours and the two next to you so I don't have any neighbors behind me.,' He sent his real estate guy on a mission to work on that."

"I was here," Bill said, "what Dave says is mostly true."

Dave looked pissed and said, "Billthy, here, needs a new place to live. Today"

I bought the place behind Dave's with a street address on Orange Grove Boulevard, a.k.a. Millionaires' Row. Kiko returned to California unexpectedly and moved into our Pasadena palace. The king of the castle, Champ, had his own wing. Every time somebody paid an exorbitant amount of money for a slice of a Honker territory I bought the place next door to our properties, and so on. Dave did the same with proceeds from his franchising of Dave's Hot Sausage restaurants all over the world. Pretty soon we owned a lot of swimming pools and guest houses.

FORTY-FIVE

THERE GOES THE NEIGHBORHOOD

PASADENA

I N A RARE MOMENT OF REFLECTION under the palm trees on Dave's massively-expanded beach, I asked Bill, "Are we out of ideas?"

"I hope so," Bill said, "the last couple of years have been exhausting."

"What are you doing with all your money? Chris told me he's handling over $20 million of your funds and you're sending most of your cash to the Bahamas."

"I don't like to spend money."

"Dave's birthday is coming up, Chris says Dave and I own too many houses."

"How is that possible?" Bill asked.

Without a great answer to all of that, I told Bill, "Because everybody has a birthday every year. You need to buy Dave the house across the street from this one and live in the guest house."

"That's not a good idea, from a business standpoint."

"You'd better do it. You've lived for free in his houses all over the world for years, he's helped you get filthy rich, it's the least you can fucking do."

"That's not a good idea."

"Bill, you've had one good idea as long as I've known you. People from Orange County are not known for good ideas—you broke the mold. The house is only $4 million. We're going to see it and you're going to buy it."

Bill did what he was told, we spent $1 million more of Bill's money to remodel the entire home, transforming it into California's greatest izakaya. Dave knew nothing about our endeavor until the grand opening/Dave's surprise birthday party.

We covered all of the windows in the grand front room with blackout curtains. Soft piano music played. A single spotlight slowly revealed a naked woman covered in sushi, sashimi, wasabi, and stuffed with edamame, on the marble kitchen island.

Then a few dozen of Dave's friends and acquaintances yelled, "Surprise!" as the bright lights and loud music signaled party time.

In the backyard, guests feasted on a magnificent buffet of delicacies Dave instantly recognized by smell. "Is Wolfgang here?" Yes, Wolfgang was there, and, just as Dave asked that, Wolfie's band launched into a blistering, mind-blowing set of rock 'n' roll that transfixed Dave and melted his face.

At the end of Wolfgang's set, Dave approached Wolfie and said, "Young man, I am thoroughly impressed. Outstanding set."

Wolfgang said, "Thank you, Dave. Fuck You. Fuck you, motherfucker. Fuck you." Bill handed Wolfie a big bag of money, Wolfgang and his posse headed to their vehicles followed by Cheesecake Factory employees close behind with more to-go boxes than Guinness had ever counted before (they counted a lot of things that night)

*Undated historical photo of a young
handsome sandwich artist. Wearing a Honker
earring. Reportedly one of Bill's ancestors.*

The ever-positive David Lee Roth shifted gears and said, "This house is somethin' else. Whose is it? I wanna commend the owner on his or her or its exquisite taste."

Bill said, "It's yours, Dave, happy birthday." And that's the first time I'd ever seen Dave cry. Dave explained how he'd bought house after house when paternity tests dictated, but nobody had ever returned the favor. Then Dave said the magic words:

"Sushi Beach."

The next morning I ran into Bill on Dave's beach. Bill was screaming into the phone, "I want every Nickelback. Every Nickelback! I will make your life fucking miserable until I get every Nickelback! Have you ever heard of the izakaya!?"

"I think you meant to say yakuza," I told Bill.

"Damn."

"Is Nickelback a big deal in Tokyo?" I asked.

"No. I was on the phone with Wolfgang's guitar company in Japan. I want every penny I paid that fat fuck returned to us, plus interest, and a penalty, in free goods for the guitar store."

"Good idea."

"That fat cunt insulted David Lee Roth."

"Are you going to charge Wolfgang for the Cheesecake Factory spread?"

"Fuck," Bill said as he redialed the guitar company in Japan. I didn't have the heart to tell Bill about the new toilet being installed after Wolfgang's blew up indestructible porcelain, and the sewer pipes under the house, let alone the sewer line under the street all the way down the hill to the arroyo. Fun fact: clay pipes were being replaced with bulletproof, kevlar-wrapped, carbon-fiber piping designed by NASA for Mars in Pasadena after Cheesecake Factory opened. Public works hadn't made it to Dave's street, yet.

FORTY-SIX

CARLITO BANDITO ON FIRE

T AZ CALLED TO INVITE KIKO AND I TO MICRONESIA to observe the majesty that is a Tropical Fuck Storm and Carlito Bandito concert extravaganza. Kiko was back in Japan working on some kind of OnlyFans thing with her twin sister, so I went alone.

"Taz! You should come help Dave turn his new house into a sushi beach."

"Fuck you. Nobody knows who Carlito Bandito is here," an angry Taz growled. "He hasn't done the groundwork. He hasn't even ever been to Pohnpei. I'm dropping him from the label."

"Taz," I said, "I've known Carlito for ten years, that badass motherfucker delivers the goods. Never underestimate the Bandito."

Taz failed to pick up what I was throwing down. "Patrick, shut the fuck up. Fuck you. Your prima donna friend, Carlito fucking Bandito, demanded to close the show. An unknown cunt like that fuck headlining above Pohnpei's Beatles? Tropical fucking Fuck Storm? Insane."

I couldn't disagree with Taz, but that didn't stop me from twisting the knife in. "Carlito is Ritchie Blackmore. Jimmy Page. He's absolutely massive in Japan. Like Godzilla. Maybe Carlito has a clinic to teach in Yokohama that day and he can't make it to Pohnpei in time for the opening slot."

"You're absolutely mental, Patrick," Taz said. "Pohnpei's a full day from anywhere, you know that. Layovers, bullshit…"

"Taz, you don't understand how much money Carlito Bandito makes in Japan," I said as I prepared to deliver the fatal blow. "Carlito owns a fighter jet. An F-5. He bought it in the Philippines. It goes over 1,000 miles an hour."

One of Carlito Bandito's problems was his inability to ever show up on time—he was always at least 15 minutes early. Weeks of intensive training prepared Carlito to begin his Pohnpei show before ever setting foot on the island. With his wireless Carlito Bandito signature model Ibanez Double-Neck Tornado fired up and ready to rock, Carlito somersaulted out of and away from his skydiving instructor's airplane and prepared to stick his landing in the middle of the floating barge known as the Honda Carlito Bandito Stage. That was the plan.

Unbeknownst to anyone at sea level, Carlito Bandito was thirty minutes early. Tropical Fuck Storm had returned from behind the wall of amplifiers on the barge/stage meant to hide their backstage fun for the traditional, exclusive to

Pohnpei, encore. The band was amused but not distracted by a parachute's appearance in the sky high above the lagoon as they hit the third verse of "For Those About to Rock."

Taz and the band knew every show at Pohnpei needed to be bigger and better. Every year the band brought something new. As the cannons fired during the third chorus of "For Those About to Rock," so did the newly refurbished World War II-era Japanese anti-aircraft guns. All assembled watched in horror and amusement as Carlito Bandito was blown out of the sky before the third *We salute you* in that third chorus. Some attributed the spectacle to Tropical Fuck Storm's conniving manager and theorized Taz had invented a fictitious act called Carlito Bandito to avoid paying another band to perform.

After the Bandito hit the water, Tropical Fuck Storm launched into a ferocious version of "Shot Down in Flames," in honor of their fallen comrade.

The late great Carlito Bandito. He was one of those about to rock. His timing was always a little bit off. We always forgave him. The crew operating the cannons and anti-aircraft weaponry, on the other hand, were exceptional timekeepers and quite unforgiving. Hence Carlito's early demise.

Maybe it was the pod of orcas Taz found at a SeaWorld liquidation sale. Or the underwater fire tornado. In any case, all that was ever recovered from the body of water now known as Carlito Bandito Lagoon was Carlito Bandito's fanny pack. Carlito Bandito, we salute you, thank you for all the amazing music you left us with. And thank you for the fanny pack full of hooker business cards and your frighteningly impressive collection of cock rings. If we can sneak a barely legal Filipina into the funeral home you'll grow and glow long into the afterlife.

Nobody at Carlito's guitar company knew what happened. I called there and posed as Carlito and told them to send every guitar possible to the Carlito Bandito Guitars store immediately. And a few to my house. A half-an-hour after Carlito's lifeless half-corpse landed in the lagoon, a bunch of little kids from the Philippines showed up in Shibuya claiming ownership of Carlito Bandito Guitars. Turns out they were right. The reason Carlito bought an old fighter jet from the Philippine air force was so he could fly from Tokyo to Manila in an hour and a half and fuck little girls. Some of those 14-year-olds who showed up in Shibuya with paternity test results in hand had 3-year-old little Banditos. Ordinarily, a 3-year-old Bandito would be cute.

Ultimately, Carlito Bandito Guitars and all of the Bandito's publishing were inherited by 35 of his offspring in the Manila area. One of his 4 year-old grandkids is said to already shred on the guitar. It must be genetic.

Back in Pasadena everybody was, understandably, bummed. My accounts of the Bandito's flaming corpse landing in the middle of a hungry orca pod were not as amusing to the people who weren't there as they remain to me. A lot of Carlito's friends did the old, "What about me?" thing and wondered about what would happen if it had been them. Let me tell you, none of those fucks had the balls to jump out of an airplane with a double-neck duct taped to their umbilical hernia the way the Bandito did.

Bill started talking about his problems, again. "I met Dave at a dam. Look, I know what you're thinking. I'm done with the randos, I hire hookers, they show up, I tell them I'm poor and that's why I live in a guest house, then I disappoint them further and further until they run away crying."

*Skydiving coach Ace (L) and the late,
great, Carlito Bandito (R and R.I.P.)*

"Dude, whatever you're talking about, that is super dark."

"Sometimes. Stop being so racist."

"Have you ever seen the belly button of the goddess Venus?"

"Is the belly button what's inside the hole or the hole itself?"

"Dude..." I said as I hit the water and remained underwater as long as I thought my iPhone would survive.

"We've all been through what you're going through before," I reassured Bill. "When Kiko goes to Japan, as soon as I confirm the plane is outbound based on the flight tracking app, and the security cameras are disabled, the hookers appear out of nowhere. Like magic. It's almost as if I have a platinum account with that service all the pornstars on Earth and the top two percent of Pasadena City College students use, or something."

"Champ told me Kiko knows all about it. She thinks it's really funny. You're lucky she loves you so much."

"Kiko has never, once, told me she loves me."

"She tells everybody she loves you."

I jumped in whatever pool we were getting hammered by so nobody could tell I was crying. "Bill, let's drop some acid, snort cocaine, eat mushrooms, and go to work at Honker Records after we finish another bottle of tequila."

"That's a great idea."

"Robbo, please. The secret weapon." Secret baseball signals were exchanged, the volume on the store's sound system was adjusted properly, and the needle dropped. Subwoofers engaged, plaster cracked and fell from the ceiling, and shoppers ran for, out, and beyond the store's exits.

Smoke Some Kill always does the trick. If Schooly D only knew. If he only knew.

FORTY-SEVEN

WAKE SOME PEOPLE UP

DAVE DEMANDED BILL AND I MEET WITH HIM for an important meeting in his bunker. The bunker can be fun, but we sensed this would not be a light-hearted event.

Bill and I arrived fifteen minutes early to find a stern-faced Dave at the head of the table who said nothing as we sat down in our assigned seats. For fifteen minutes we sat there in silence with dramatic lighting until 9 a.m. when the video monitors came to life revealing Taz in Australia.

Dave said, "We don't know shit!" loud as fuck. "We don't know shit! One fucking scientist studies giraffes and tells us what giraffes are all about and everybody thinks we know every fucking thing we ever need to know about giraffes."

"Was the scientist Neil de—"

"Every giraffe is different! My dogs are from the same litter—completely different from each other, insane little bastards. We don't know a goddamned motherfucking thing about anything!"

I said, "That's the first step, Dave."

"Fuck you, Dick Patrick. Fuck you. I wanna know how we can fight stupid. Fix stupid. Fuck stupid. Forget stupid."

"So, you wanna fight it, fix it, fuck it, forget it? That's the 4F Club," I told Dave the day he discovered The Mentors.

"Gentlemen! The time has come," Dave screamed. "We have had our fun, we have made millions, the time has come."

Bill said, "I—"

"Silence!" Dave screamed at Bill before he could ask a stupid question. "All of the money we have made has been made doing stupid shit. We need to piss some people off. Wake some people up. Burn some shit down, Blow some shit up. Metaphorically speaking, of course. What can we do to wake people up? I want ideas by 9 a.m. tomorrow."

The video monitors went blank. The lights in the bunker went dark, save for the one in the exit stairwell.

"Get out!" screamed the meeting's host.

FORTY-EIGHT

GO GET HER!
GO GET HER!

B ARNEY'S. The beanery. The barn show. Barney's big bad beanery. Bill interrupted my derailed train of thought, "Dude, you should go to Japan."

"I've been thinking about it."

"You need to go to Japan."

"Maybe when Kiko gets back we'll—"

"Motherfucker! Go to Japan! Go. To. Japan! Go see Kiko! All she does there is talk about you, you stupid motherfucker. Go see her!"

I walked outside and stared at the sky.

FUCK THIS PLANET

FUCK THESE PEOPLE

FUCK IT ALL

FUCK IT ALL

Back at home I jumped into one of my swimming pools and remained underwater until I ran out of tears. Then I left home without telling anyone where I was going. It was either a bridge or a cliff or an airport with airplanes that fly to faraway places. Nobody needed to know. I've been to the edge.

You're a millionaire in America and you're unhappy.
YES, I AM! FUCK THIS SHIT!
FUCK ALL OF THESE FUCKING FUCKS!

From the edge of the Colorado Street Bridge, I called Taz, for some reason. Maybe because I thought Japan was near Australia.

"I need a vacation, Taz."

"Go to Japan."

"Why?"

"Kiko is there."

"Kiko? I've been thinking about—"

"Kiko, you stupid motherfucker. Are you a fucking idiot? Jesus fucking Christ. You're the dumbest motherfucker I know. Go see Kiko! Nobody will ever fucking care about any of the stupid shit you are doing right now. Nobody will ever care about you as much as Kiko cares about you. It makes me sick. She's totally fucking gone. It makes no sense. Kiko doesn't fucking need you. She's a badass with or without you"

I knew all of my friends were insane people who could not be trusted. I went to Japan, anyway, to see how Honker was doing.

On the way from the airport to Shibuya, I found a flower shop and bought a few red roses to hide behind as I entered Honker Records. I see right through distorted eyes.

It had been a while. It had also been a while since I'd seen Kiko. Part of me wanted to run away before she noticed me. That part of me isn't an important part of me. Nobody will ever let you know when you ask the reasons why. They just tell you that you're on your own and fill your head all full of lies. Tony Iommi wouldn't do that..

The second greatest Black Sabbath record was blasting the brains out of nine floors of Japanese people when I walked into Honker Records. The sound was magnificently loud and thick as fuck. Epic. A salesperson asked me a question in Szechuan or something like that, I said "No hablan Español," which was and remains 100% true. A mean little sexy woman appeared out of nowhere and slapped the Honker frown right off of my face and screamed, "You bastards!" at the same time Ozzy did, right before the guitar solo. I was almost over *Sabbath Bloody Sabbath* before that.

The world paused and stopped and ended and started all over again in slow motion all sped up and processed through foot pedals with massive amounts of saturation before it hit the analog board and went upside down to the parallel processor dude who fired two channels right up into my skull while two more secret agent outputs reverberated off of plates and springs and all kinds of awesome nonsense at the same time.

Kiko and I walked out of Honker Records for the last time and never looked back. We left all of the roses at the Carlito Bandito Memorial his 37 children installed, save the one Kiko kept.

A couple of weeks after we returned from Japan, Honker visited me in a dream. Honker flew into my office as I was weighing a few hundred pounds of $100 bills and said, "Domo arigato, Pato-chan. Domo arigato."

Honker was telling me he was happy and grateful for the new life we gave him as the ultimate symbol of awesomeness in Japan. I was happy for that motherfucker, Honker, for a moment, until I asked myself *Why the fuck didn't we use Black Patrick's face on that skyscraper?*

Honker claims he is not fucking Hello Kitty.
I believe him. Honker is allergic to cats.

FORTY-NINE

WE MUST NEVER BE APART

EVER AFTER

I DIDN'T NEED TO BE HERE TONIGHT. With my vast financial holdings, I could be basking in the sun in Florida. The words spoken by Richard Manitoba on The Dictators *Go Girl Crazy* in the late 1970s had never been more prescient.

We fired up the sound system, turned up The Dictators, lit shit on fire, and slapped burgers on Dave's beach grill. Bill said, "Dude, you look like shit."

"I feel like shit, too," I said. "I'm all fucked up, man."

"The election?"

"Yeah, but it's mostly Kiko. I'm not really sure…"

"Not really sure about what? She's perfect."

"I'm not sure she's of age if you know what I mean."

"That would suck, man. Do you think she's jailbait?"

"I'm not convinced she isn't."

"You're worried she's 17 or under?"

"Yes. Yes, in all honesty, I really am."

"I'll find out."

A minute or so later Bill returned. "She's 37."

"Aw, fuck. That's even worse."

"Her daughter's 19."

"Don't even say it, you fucking—"

"Her daughter's kid—"

And that was the very moment I discovered I was about to wed somebody's grandmother.

Because I think I'm funny, the night before the greatest day of her life, I told a woman, "Kiko, if you're seeing any red flags or future nightmares with me you need to end it all right now. I don't want you to get hurt."

Kiko looked me in the eye, then she looked down at my penis in her hand, and then she laughed.

The only officiant we could find willing and able to perform at our wedding was former funnyman, Ron White. "Patrick, Kiko, people think you're crazy. Together, when with each other, you don't feel crazy." Kiko started crying and the tears exited through her nostrils. Happens every time.

"You two add something to each other, so magically and effortlessly. You serve each other and the union between you. Your connection is subconscious and permanent. You are strong enough to be brutally honest with each other. You are not on the same death trip. Most of the time."

Our assembled friends and family laughed, shared flasks, and made jokes with each other.

"For those about to rock, before the groom gropes his much younger bride, we will listen to their unprepared vows. Kiko, please begin."

Kiko and Black Patrick get married.

Kiko:	Patrick, I will give you everything I have.
Patrick:	Kiko, you will be the happiest woman in the world.
Kiko:	We will make beautiful music together.
Patrick:	Our beautiful music will be amplified.
Kiko:	Our music will make dogs howl, neighbors angry.
Patrick:	Our home will have bullet holes in the windows.
Kiko:	We must never be apart.

Patrick:	We will wander aimlessly together.
Kiko:	You will never question my love.
Patrick:	Where have you been all my life?
Kiko:	You make me fearless.
Patrick:	You scare the shit out of me.
Kiko:	My name is Britney.
Patrick:	Hit me, baby, one more time.

The slap-activated rock 'n' roll machine blasted Howlin Wolf's "Killing Floor" prematurely; assembled friends and family took that as a cue to make a beeline for the party bus outside Dave's compound—Barney's Beanery awaited. Eventually, Kiko and I joined our beloved posse at the reception. We kept going with the back-and-forth vows until we couldn't stand it anymore:

You have me to hold your hand.
You have me to understand.
You will dream of me at night.
I will thrill you with delight.
I'm gonna love you each and every day.
Wild horses couldn't drag me away.
Wild horses couldn't drag me away.
Wild horses couldn't drag me away.
We are the champions.
Rock me like a hurricane.
Always and forever.
Love will keep us together.
Love will keep us together.
Always and forever.

Black Patrick lives in Los Angeles, writes books, and remains scarred by the one and only encounter with his childhood hero, Memphis Slim.